Backbeat

A Bombs Away Mystery

E.S. Sargent

PopPulp

Contents

Chapter 1

Thursday, September 4th, 1986, 5:00 p.m.

Sweat dripped down my forehead and into my eyes, blurring my vision until I blinked them clear. I surveyed the club we were playing, squinting through the bright lights. It was a tiny place that would hold a couple hundred people if the fire inspector was paid off. Tonight, it had about forty. *Who comes to a punk show on a Thursday afternoon?*

Tom's voice rang out over the speakers.

"I'm Tom, lead singer of this ragtag gang." His tall fan mohawk towered over him, adding about eight inches to his height. I swear that was the real reason he had it that way. It was dyed bright blue that night, but you could never guess what color it would be from show to show.

Tom stood out front like a bulldog protecting his home. Little did that crowd know he'd run if they said, "Boo." He was more like a chihuahua most days.

"Over here to my right is the one, the only, *Sam*!" Tom gestured to her with both hands, like a magician revealing his assistant.

Sam stood at six foot two, and every inch of her a blond bombshell. We never understood why she still stuck around with us. She had other choices: modeling, acting… Well, maybe not acting. She'd need to say more than two words to someone other than us to do that. Her head was shaved on one side, the rest long and swept over half her face. Safety pins pierced her ear in three or four places and glinted in the lights. When she did talk, she had an accent, but we could never figure out where it came from.

After Tom said her name, she thumped out a few complicated runs on her bass. Music was how she truly communicated with the world.

"Last but not least, my friend and the backbeat, the backbone of this whole thing: *Sticks*!"

When he said my name, I raised my drumsticks, screamed, 'Bombs Away!' and clapped them together. 'One! Two! Three! Four!

A burst of adrenaline rushed through me. Bombs Away belonged up on the stage, performing for anyone who would listen. Launching into the song, I pounded out rhythms on the drums. From my spiky hair to my ratty *Misfits* T-shirt, I embodied the punk stereotype. It was never about the fashion for me though; it was the music. I let it take over and slammed my drumsticks down with every fiber of my being.

A small group made their way to the front and gathered around the stage. Even though the crowd was too thin to mosh, they all danced with everything they had. I guess if you came to see a band before dark in the middle of the week, you were really into it.

Tom's voice kicked in and started the lyrics. Playing on autopilot, my hands kept rhythm while my mind wandered.

This place is a ghost town. The scent of unwashed bodies and cigarettes doesn't help either. Why are we doing this? Traveling from Milwaukee to Canada for a tiny audience like this.

Our manager Charlie had us doing this all the time. He called it "paying your dues." Driving fourteen hours to Canada once a month was paying something, but I think "the dues" felt a little too high.

Everyone was jumping to the beat. Across the stage, I caught a glimpse of Sam shredding the four strings of her instrument. A lot of eyes were on her and not Tom. I wondered if she ever thought about leaving the band. Was she okay playing mediocre clubs forever?

That was the first time I'd thought the words "leave the band."

I forced myself back, focusing on every strike of my drumsticks, and let everything else fall away. Tom stood at the front, one foot propped up on the monitor, playing a solo. He was a silhouette before me, a wiry little punk with a glowing mohawk. He made his way back to the mic and started to shout out the chorus.

The crowd pumped their fists in the air. At least they were here for it. I let the crowd's energy fill me up, recharging me. The volume kept climbing until the song crashed to a halt, and the crowd cheered for us. *Punk never rests.* We only hesitated for a moment before I called out, "One! two! three! four!" and launched right into the next tune.

My forearms burned as I put everything I had into each song. Still, my mind drifted. Memories started forcing their way in. The long drives and the perpetual battle to keep the band afloat. Rinse and repeat. When was the last time we had a real break? An opportunity that didn't fall through or end in disaster?

We started this band with visions of anarchy and rebellion. It wasn't a whole lot of that anymore, but the struggle—the struggle to keep playing, to make enough to survive? That was punk too. The shine might have washed off, the dream now tarnished and dented, but we were out there making music, and we were together. That was all we'd ever asked for. I should be able to be happy with that, but I wasn't.

I can't do this anymore, I realized. *I'm done.* I reached down deep and let myself go one last time.

Out in the small crowd, a lone figure caught my eye. He stumbled and swayed as he made his way to the front, determined to get to us. As he reached the stage, he started to climb onto it. *Oh, no. Here we go.*

Every once in a while, we had a brave soul who wanted to stage dive. Usually, you wanted more people out there to catch you. I hoped he had insurance. Instead of turning around to dive, he started making his way in Sam's direction. She acted like she hadn't even seen him yet. The drunk was mouthing something, but I couldn't make it out over the sound of us playing. The lewd gesture he made with his hand told me everything I needed to know.

I smiled. This was about to get interesting.

She didn't glance up but pivoted to the side as he approached. The drunk lunged at her. In one smooth motion, she shuffled a step back, lifted a foot, and *kicked*. The drunk went sailing through the air as the song reached a natural pause. He hit the ground with a sickening thud and sharp exhalation of air as all the wind was knocked out of him.

The music flooded back in as we played our way through the last couple of bars. Nobody messed with Sam. Ever. She never even missed a note.

The gaps closed back in around the drunk. He stood up, holding his side and made his way to the back. *That'll sober you up real quick.*

The rest of the afternoon passed by in an uneventful blur. By the end, my arms were tingling, and we were all sweat-soaked and tired.

"Thank you, Winnipeg. You've been fantastic!" Tom yelled into his mic as we crashed out the final note.

I moved out from behind my kit and made my way to the front of the stage. We wrapped our arms around each other and gave a final bow to all forty of our "adoring" fans.

"That was some kick," Tom said, patting Sam on the shoulder.

She shrugged. "He didn't say *please*."

Tom and I both laughed as Sam moved to start packing up her bass. We finished putting away our gear and wrapping up cables. A few people stopped by to say thanks before filtering out. We headed to the bar with a familiar post-show rush that made the exhaustion melt away for a moment.

"Drinks are on me!" said Lena as we approached. "You guys were amazing tonight. You need to tell Charlie to book you on a weekend."

"Tell me about it," I said, trying to keep all the frustration out of my voice.

"Sweet kick, Sam," Lena said with her eyebrows raised, ever hopeful she'd get a response.

Sam smiled and gave a single nod in return.

"I'm going to crack through that thin candy shell someday, I swear to god. In any case, that guy deserved it." Lena counted out some bills from the register and handed them to Tom. "Sorry it's not more."

I shrugged along with Tom. It would pay the rent, but barely.

She poured us each a drink that we lifted in the air.

"To Bombs Away. May we never stop raising hell," Tom said with a grin and slugged back his drink.

Sam and I joined him, smiling at the familiar toast.

"To Bombs Away," Lena said as she also took a drink. "Canada will always welcome its thirty-seventh favorite American punk band whose name starts with the letter B."

"For that, we're going to need another drink," I said, clutching my chest as if run through by her sharp wit. She liked to bust our chops, but I knew she liked us and our music; I was sure of that.

At the same time though, I couldn't help but think that this would probably be the last time we played together.

Chapter 2

Thursday, September 4th, 1986, 6:32 p.m.

The club's smokey haze was clearing up, but the scent of tobacco that had caused it still clung to my nostrils. I nodded to Lena, who was busy cleaning the bar in preparation for the next show, "Can I use your phone? I need to check in with Charlie."

She jerked a thumb in the direction of the far wall, saying, "Go for it."

I made my way to the black Bakelite phone hanging on a wall covered in graffiti and stickers. I picked it up and spun out Charlie's number on the rotary dial, waiting as it turned back into place after every number.

Tom was talking and laughing with Lena on the other side of the room, Sam stood nearby smiling silently. I turned my back to them so I could try to have a private word with Charlie. The phone only rang twice before he picked up.

"What's shakin', bacon?" Charlie's smarmy tone was as evident as ever.

"Charlie, it's Sticks. Just finished up here." I forced myself to sound as upbeat as possible. The adrenaline of the stage started to leave my body. An ache and a weariness replaced it.

"Sticks, my boy. Fantastic. I'm sure it was as amazing as ever. Sorry I couldn't be there. Busy, busy, busy," Charlie said. In my mind, his hands moved around as he talked. He communicated as much with them as he did with his mouth.

"Charlie," I began, lowering my voice, "I need to speak to you when we're ba—"

"Sticks, listen," he interrupted, his words tumbling out with excitement. "I've got news—huge news! I landed you a show at The Palms. It's a proper venue. You're going to be headlining. There's even going to be a couple of record execs."

"Wait, what?" my mind trying to latch on to what he had said. I was trying to make sense of it. "We're going to play at *The* Palms? With record execs?"

"Damn straight," Charlie confirmed, his enthusiasm infectious. "This is it, Sticks. This Saturday. The Palms. Rehearsal and sound check tomorrow afternoon at the venue. In two days, when you knock 'em dead, everything changes."

"We'll be back as soon as we can," I managed to say, "Thanks, Charlie. This is huge. We'll head out right away."

"Sounds great, kid. Say hello to Liam for me when you're at the border. Tell him to give his wife and kids my best." Liam was Charlie's buddy who worked at the crossing. I was glad Charlie wasn't here. It would have taken twice as long to make it home if he had been with us. He'd talk Liam's ear off any chance he got.

"Will do, Charlie." I hung up the receiver and tried to steady my breathing. My heart was threatening to break out of my ribcage and make a run for it. I took one more breath in and let it out, spinning back around to face the bar.

"Change of plans," I called out while walking back to the group. My need to talk to Charlie and leave the band had moved to the back of my mind. "We landed a gig at The Palms. We're headlining, and rumor has it record execs will be there."

"Are you for real?" Tom asked while Sam's eyes widened in surprise.

"Absolutely." The rush of anticipation filled me, "We need to pack up and hit the road. Rehearsal is tomorrow, and we need to be on our way."

"Damn right!" Tom shouted, high-fiving Sam as they headed toward the equipment and started to move it toward our ride parked outside.

I waved to Lena. "Thanks for the beers," I said as I picked up some cables and part of my drum kit. "We'll let you know how it goes. We've got to keep our number one fan up to date."

"You better. I can't wait to find out how much ass you kicked." Lena smiled as she said it and started to wipe down the bar top with a rag.

I made my way outside with my armload of stuff, setting it down beside the van as I approached.

It was an all-black 1972 Dodge Tradesman. The paint was peeling all around the edges, which happened when you used cheap house paint on a vehicle. We'd painted our logo—a giant round cartoon bomb with a lit fuse. The word "Bombs" was in curved letters above it, and the word "Away!" was opposite that on the bottom. The new spare tire Charlie had installed on the back door last summer was the nicest thing about it.

We made a couple of trips to load the stuff. The sound of the drums and cymbals crashing as we set them down rang out like a battle cry. I walked around to the other side to make sure we hadn't left anything on the ground.

A disheveled, grimy man lumbered around the back of the van toward the street. He didn't act drunk, but he was still stumbling and unsteady. It was getting dark a little earlier, so the streetlights had kicked on, but slivers of sunlight still colored the sky. The man stepped onto the street right as I caught some movement out of the corner of my eye.

"Watch out!" I shouted as I sprinted to him. I reached out, grabbing his arm as I got close, and pulled him back onto the curb.

He turned to me in surprise as a car sped past him, our clothes fluttering in the wind its passage caused.

"Jesus, that was close," I muttered, my pulse pounding in my temples from the near miss.

The man's eyes, bloodshot and bulging with shock, were swiveling around, trying to piece together what had just happened.

"Thanks, kid," he rasped, leaning against me for support. "You saved my life."

"Least I could do." I pulled a few crumpled dollar bills out of my pocket and pressed them into his hand. "Grab some food and a warm place to sleep tonight."

"Bless you," he whispered when he reached out to grab the bills. I could see his arms were covered in tattoos; there were even some peeking out of the collar of his shirt. Snakes of all shapes and sizes. He clutched the money close with his greasy hands and waved at me again as I returned to my bandmates.

"Everything cool, Sticks?" Tom asked, his voice filled with concern.

"Nothing to worry about," I said, brushing off the incident with a grin. "Had a close one, that's all."

"Bravo, well done," Sam said, clapping me on the shoulder. Her voice was as mysterious as ever, but that was high praise from her.

"We need to go," I realized as I glanced at my watch. "We've got some miles to cover."

With our equipment safely stored away, we settled into our seats. The familiar musty stink of the van's rotting upholstery settled around us. Tom turned the key in the ignition, The engine stubbornly but dependably rumbled back to life.

"Bombs Away," Tom said, fiddling with the radio dials. "Next stop: Milwaukee." He put it in gear and pulled away from the curb.

The events of the night replayed in my mind. I was excited about what was coming and felt guilty about my earlier doubts. It must have been written all over my face.

Tom cleared his throat, side-eyeing me, "You good?"

"Never better," I said, forcing the guilt back down. "Let's go home."

"Here's to making it big!" Tom said as he drove down the street, leaving the club behind.

"Damn right!" I found myself more confident by the minute. The drive ahead was long, but all that mattered was getting there and showing everyone what Bombs Away was made of.

It only took us an hour or so before we rolled up to the border crossing. The lights illuminating all the signs flickered. We rolled down the windows, and they buzzed loud enough, almost to drown out the rumble of the road beneath us.

We pulled into the far-left lane, knowing it was where Liam always was. He stepped out of his booth, a weary smile on his face. He must be getting close to the end of his shift.

"Tom! Bombs Away. Right on schedule!" Liam called out, waving us up to the booth. He knew us well with all the trips we'd made through his checkpoint. He seemed to like us, but I didn't think he'd ever been to one of our gigs.

"Yo, Liam!" I called out as he approached the window. "Charlie says hello and to give your wife and kids his best."

"Ah, Charlie," Liam said, the bags under his eyes darkening by the second. "So thoughtful. Let me check things over real fast, and you'll be on your way."

"Do your thing, Liam! " Tom piped up. "We've got a date with destiny!"

Liam chuckled and started doing his routine check, the same one he'd done a few hours ago when we got here. It was busier then, so he didn't have time to chat.

"I spied the new logo this morning when you came through," he called out from behind us where we didn't have a view of him. He was checking around under the vehicle with a mirror attached to his shoe. Metal clanged against metal as he tapped the end of his flashlight on various parts of the van. "It's awesome."

"Yeah, we thought it was time for an upgrade." Tom smiled. "Find anything more interesting than our painting skills?"

"Just the normal wear and tear," Liam said, then finished with, "Okay, you're ready to go!" He bumped his fist on the side panel a couple of times. "Enjoy your date with destiny, Tom," Liam said as he strode away from us. "I hope she's real pretty."

"But—" Tom tried to interrupt and stopped, realizing Liam was already back in his booth. "Whatever." He chuckled and took off through the border crossing.

With the remainder of a fourteen-hour drive in front of us, we rotated our favorite tapes through the crappy sound system. I tried not to get my hopes too high about The Palms and what it meant for us. It was hard, though; my mind was running wild with all the possibilities of what was to come.

The sun was well up in the sky before the outline of Milwaukee came into view. Sam was at the wheel as we'd all taken turns driving to make it home as soon as possible. I couldn't wait to get some real sleep that wasn't cramped in the van, even if it was on my worn-out old cot.

The city fell in around us as we drove our way through the streets to the warehouse district. The acrid odor of tanneries mixed with the sickly sweetness of the breweries was something you didn't miss, but you couldn't forget it either.

"Smells like home," Tom grumbled from the back seat as he stirred awake.

Sam pulled around the last few streets and into the narrow driveways surrounding the warehouse we called home. We piled out and lugged our equipment inside with a slow shuffle. We didn't want it stolen right before the night that would change everything.

"I can't wait to get some sleep on that terrible cot," I said, speaking my earlier thoughts aloud.

"My lumpy couch is calling my name." Tom yawned, still half asleep.

Sam shrugged. She had the only bedroom and a real bed. I still didn't know where she got it from. I remembered her lugging the mattress through the door by herself one day. I was sure Tom and I would have struggled to do that together.

We finished stowing the equipment in a locked closet on the ground floor. The rest of the expansive space was empty and unused. Light filtered in through the many windows in giant slanting beams. The long-empty building was cavernous and echoed our footsteps and the clanking of equipment being stowed. Far across the empty concrete expanse, you could make out the line of garage bay doors we were too lazy to use. It was easier to park outside the small door that was closest to our apartment.

We made our way up the flight of metal stairs to what I could only assume used to be the office for the building. I fumbled with the keys and opened the locks.

The door swung inward to reveal our shabby apartment—the cot over in the corner and a threadbare couch, the door to Sam's room, and our industrial sink, mini fridge, and hot plate kitchen. The picture of luxury. Still, we all sighed with relief, made our way to our beds, and flopped onto them.

"Good night, everyone," I said to the room.

"You mean good morning," Sam corrected from her bedroom.

Tom chuckled as he settled in to fall asleep.

The clattering of dishes jolted me awake. Across the room Tom also sat straight up at the same time.

"Shit. Rehearsal!" Tom cried out.

Sam was already dressed and was putting a pan away after making breakfast. Eggs were steaming on plates at the center of the table. She shook her head at us both.

We should have known better; she would have kept us from being late. We shoveled the food into our mouths, most of it even got there. I used my hand to sweep up anything that had missed its target onto my plate and chucked it all into the sink. Cleanup would have to be a tomorrow problem.

We loaded the equipment back up and piled in to head out. I got behind the driver's seat and stuck the key in the ignition. Sam was sitting shotgun, Tom in the back in what we referred to as the "gunner's seat," which was just an old bus seat we'd salvaged and welded to the floor.

I glanced over my shoulder at Tom. He had a mad Cheshire grin on his face. "Let's *do this*!" he screamed, punching the roof a couple of times with his fist.

I cranked the engine and stomped on the gas. The vehicle shuttered and then sputtered to a stop. "Shit."

I could feel Tom's eyes on me. I turned the key successfully this time, then steered us north over the river to the downtown location.

"No detours this time," Tom said, chuckling from behind me.

"That was one time, man," I said, giving him a mock hard glare in the mirror. "Mostly because your directions were garbage."

"Sure, blame it on me," he scoffed, rolling his eyes.

We lurched slowly and steadily into downtown traffic. After a few minutes of making turns through the streets, our destination appeared a little ahead: an old theater renovated into a modern music venue.

The Palms had become quite the hotspot in recent years. A lot of people had gotten their first break there, then moved on to bigger and better things. I was hopeful we might be next.

"Okay, guys. Here we go," I said to my friends around me. "This is going to change everything!"

Tom was grinning in the mirror. Sam sat stoic next to me, but I glanced over and saw the tiniest smile on her face. Even she couldn't hold it back.

Charlie's voice rang in my head. *In two days, when you knock 'em dead, everything changes.*

Chapter 3

Friday, September 5th, 1986, 2:16 p.m.

The open sign in the window buzzed like a dying fly as we stormed through the front door to The Palms. This was our temple, our battleground. We fully intended to blow the roof off this place. Bombs Away, ready to detonate.

It didn't need to be said, but I was excited. Tom pulled me out of it real quick.

"Sticks? It's spooky quiet in here." His voice betrayed him, trembling as he said it.

I stopped to take it in. It *was* quiet. I clutched my drumsticks like two lifelines. My eyes found Sam. She sensed it, too. She was as close as a person could be to a cat with its hackles standing up.

"Too quiet." I had to hand it to him. He sniffed out trouble like a bloodhound. It was his body's defense mechanism.

Tom stood there, actually shaking in his boots. Now I realized where that saying came from. Even his mohawk wasn't immune; the shaking of his body made it quiver along with the rest of him.

"This is wrong," Sam said, sounding like she was also on edge, which was no easy feat. She was illuminated by the sunlight streaming in the front door. Bass slung over her shoulder, both hands clutching the strap. Her head swiveled around as she took in everything around us.

It was afternoon. Someone should have been here setting up the bar or cleaning, doing something, anything. Instead, it was like a mausoleum, save for the hum coming from the old jukebox as it spun another forty-five in place and let the needle drop. A Bowie song started, filling the space with sound.

"Where is everybody?" I said, almost under my breath. My eyes scanned the interior. My grip tightened on my drumsticks, and my knuckles went white. The stage was in front of us, like a promise and a threat all at once.

"Maybe everyone is late today?" Tom suggested, but he didn't sound like he believed that at all. He pulled back as a rat skittered across the floor to his right. "What the hell!" he cried out. Then, his cheeks reddened, embarrassed that it had made him jump.

"Something is wrong," Sam said, her one uncovered blue eye looking at each of us. She had this way about her; if something went down, it was all business.

"Let's check the green room." I motioned to the two of them as I stepped further inside. We made our way toward the corridor beside the stage. It was lined with stickers, graffiti, and ancient set lists from bands I recognized. My boots stuck to the beer-stained floor, inching toward whatever waited for us.

"Stay together." Sam's voice rang out in the silence. It was a command, not a suggestion.

"Wouldn't dream of splitting up," Tom replied shakily. It was no sweat to face any crowd, guitar and mic between him and the world. Darkness and silence, though? That was a different animal altogether.

I placed my hand on the doorknob and turned, the click of the latch ringing out like a gunshot in the quiet around us. I paused with the door barely open a crack. The memory of a nightmare slithered through me—standing in front of a packed house, getting ready to start a song none of us knew. At least I wasn't naked this time.

"Ready?" I said, not ready myself and unsure what I was expecting to see on the other side of the door.

"Always," Tom squeaked.

Sam gave a single nod.

We plunged through the door into complete darkness. It was like a bunker with no windows back here.

"Charlie, this isn't funny, man!" I called out into the black.

I wished he would answer me, jump out, and say this was all just a joke. I ran my hands along the wall beside the door, looking for a light switch.

When I found it, I flipped it up to the on position. A flood of light filled the room, and I lurched backward. My mind reeling with a scene too gruesome to comprehend.

Charlie lay sprawled out before us on the cold concrete, a twisted sculpture in a cheap business suit. A blood-smeared drumstick jutted from his eye socket, macabre and surreal. His other eye stared blankly at the three of us.

My pulse was thundering in my temples. This was no joke. This was real. This was happening.

This was murder.

"Who would do this to Charlie?" Tom choked out. He was gagging like he was about to throw up.

"I don't know," I snapped back, my mind racing. A killer was on the loose, and we were standing in the middle of his greatest hit.

Sam circled the room, taking it all in. Cold, calculating. When she got to the opposite side of Charlie's body, she inhaled with a sharp sucking sound. Her eyes shot open in shock.

"What is it?" I asked. I was circling to meet her. My eyes followed hers to the drumstick. Then I saw it. Clear as day, my name scrawled on the side of it. Smeared with sweat, then blood.

I remembered the day I gave that to Charlie. He'd taken us on as clients and had me sign it. "You're gonna be famous, kid. I want the first autograph," he'd told me. I believed every word of it.

Sam was down on the floor, close to the body now, but not touching anything.

"Sam, how can you?" Tom questioned from the far side of the room. Still hugging the door, hand over his mouth. "I can't do this. Charlie, man... He's..."

"Keep it together, Tommy," I hissed, even though my own hands were shaking.

Sam was cut from a different cloth. She got closer, peering at the drumstick, then investigated the rest of his body, hands clasped behind her back but bent over at the waist to get as close a look as possible.

Sam cleared her throat when she got close. She unclasped her hands and held the back of one to her nostrils. "Someone did this, Tom. I intend to find out who. Getting sick won't help."

"Right, sick," Tom muttered, keeping his hand over his mouth like the word itself might trigger his stomach.

"Sam's right, Tom." I nodded to her, trying to pull him back from the edge. "She's got a point. We need to keep our heads."

"Easy for her to say," he spat out, trying and failing to keep it together. "I think she's done this kind of thing before."

"Wouldn't surprise me," I murmured more to myself than to him. Sam's past was a locked case, and best of luck finding the key.

"We need to not be here right now," Tom told us, and I agreed.

Sam peered into every corner of the place for any clues as to who did this. The room wasn't all that big but had clutter everywhere. Shoving aside the cracked and dry leather couch she looked for anything that might have found its way underneath. With a flick of her wrist, she motioned to some blood spattered on the floor near Charlie, a warning not to step in it. Finally, she made her way back over to his body and knelt down beside it again.

"He's right. We shouldn't take too long," I pleaded with her, worried we'd already spent too much time.

She ignored me, fished into her pocket, and pulled out a handkerchief. She reached forward toward one of Charlie's hands.

"Sam, what are you…" I started to ask.

She held up her other hand to silence me and continued to reach forward. She used the handkerchief to pull something from Charlie's hand and pocketed it.

"Okay," she said. Her accent thickened. "Now we make it like we were never here. Wipe off anything you touched." She went around the room, scuffing up dust that might betray footprints.

I used my shirt to wipe off the light switch and copied her shuffling around in the dust. Tom just stood still, unmoving, eyes bulging.

"Now," Sam said, "we go."

You didn't have to tell us twice; we went out the door, wiping the handles behind us. As I headed outside, I turned back to look at Charlie's body. His one eye stared at me as I shut the door behind us.

We went to the back door and popped out behind the building. I pushed ahead of the group and made my way through the alley. In my hurried pace, I tripped over a bottle and sent it clattering against the wall. It shattered into a million pieces, the light sparkling off it like little diamonds.

"Shit," I cursed at my two left feet. My head swiveled around. Every shadow was a cop. Every sound was the killer coming to finish me off.

We circled around and hopped into our van, trying to act as normal as possible. We lucked out; no one was walking around the streets today. I stopped in my tracks with my hand on the door. *Why is there no one around?* It was like someone had just told everyone not to come to work today. Sam got behind the wheel, and the engine roared to life, pulling me out of my thoughts. I got in shotgun, and Tom settled into the gunner seat. We tore through the city.

"We need to call the cops," Tom said behind us. "Why aren't we calling the cops?"

"We can't," I said, "You stayed on the other side of the room and didn't see it. That drumstick has my name on it. They're going to pin this thing on me."

"Oh god, Charlie..." Tom croaked his hand back over his mouth again. "What are we going to do? I can't handle this."

"Tommy, I need you, man," I said, trying to calm him down if that was possible. "I'm scared too, but we need to know who did this. When the police find that drumstick, they'll trace it to me. They're not going to pass go. They're not going to collect two hundred dollars. They'll just throw me in jail."

He swallowed hard. His leather jacket creaked as he shifted around, uncomfortable. "Sticks, I... I don't know, man..."

"You don't know what?" I said harsher than I meant to. "You don't know if you can stand up for your friend? I need your help on this."

"I'll try," Tom promised, "but you saw him, man. What they did to him? It's like something out of those trashy horror flicks we watch."

I turned to him and stared right into his eyes. "Help me prove this wasn't me."

He hesitated, grappling with everything that was going on. He sighed. "Of course, man. We're in this together."

Sam was driving with determination, her jaw clenched.

"What did you find, Sam?" I said, trying to pull her out of whatever thoughts were racing around in her head. "On Charlie. What did you pick up?"

She reached into her pocket, pulled out the handkerchief, and handed it to me. I opened it up to peer inside at the contents. It was a tiny bag of white powder with a picture of a snake eating its tail—a snake with black, yellow, and red stripes.

"Are these drugs? Since when was Charlie into this stuff?" I wondered aloud.

"He either always was, or someone wanted us to think he was," Sam replied without her eyes leaving the road.

We rumbled along quiet streets, a monstrosity of rust and rebellion that had seen better days. We'd all seen better days.

I broke the silence. "Do we even know anyone who deals? Anyone who would know more about this?"

"Mick or Spike might," Tommy croaked, referring to a couple of other guys we knew from the scene. "They like to party more than the average bear."

"So Mick or Spike. That's a start," I said, doing my best impression of every cop movie I'd ever seen. "Are we doing this? Are we going to try and figure this out?"

Tom shrugged behind me, still unsure. "This sucks, but you're right, Sticks. When they find that drumstick, they'll try to pin this on you. Even if they had no evidence, they'd be after us. We're one of his only clients."

"We talk to Mick and try to find Spike. What else?"

"His office. We might find more info in his file cabinets or something," Tom said, his wits returning to him.

"We're close to the office. Let's hit that. Then we can try to find Spike. We should call Lena too. She might know something about Charlie we didn't?" I did my best to sound as confident as possible. The only thing that betrayed that confidence was my constant checking behind us for flashing lights. Every siren in the distance was someone coming for us.

"It's a plan." Sam shrugged. "Part of one, anyway."

I sat in silence for the rest of the ride, my mind running through the last few days. My paranoia came and went as I rationalized the events and our actions. Over and over again, I went back to Charlie on the phone during our last conversation.

In two days, when you knock 'em dead, everything changes.

Well, you were wrong about that, Charlie. You were dead wrong. It only took one.

Chapter 4

Friday, September 5th, 1986, 3:48 p.m.

The late afternoon sunlight flashed off the various buildings, hitting our eyes at random moments. I attempted to adjust the sunshades in the front seat with no luck. I squinted around us at the dirty streets and garbage-filled alleyways.

We pulled into an unused driveway about a block away and got out to walk the rest of the way to the building. The three of us were on edge, our nerves frayed as we made our way down the back street.

"Man, this place always gives me the creeps," Tom muttered, glancing around nervously while his shoulders slumped. His eyes darted around, nervous and searching.

"Just breathe, Tommy," I said, my hands shoved deep into my pockets. "We're here for Charlie." In the back of my mind, I was thinking, *For me, too.*

Sam moved like a shadow, her boots padding along, making almost no sound. The sunlight reflected off the shaved side of her head as she craned her neck to see down the alleys we passed.

"Here we go," I said, my eyes darting over the nondescript brick walls of Charlie's place. It was about as inviting as a prison. I wanted to go in and search for more information, but I couldn't bring myself to do it yet. There were too many memories and not enough answers. "I'm going to call Lena to see if she knows anything that will help."

I made my way over to the payphone on the corner. Shabby, covered in graffiti and a layer of chewed bubblegum, it matched the neighborhood like it had always been this way. I pulled change from my pockets and put a few quarters in. I punched in Lena's number.

"Come on, Lena," I urged as it rang.

"Wellington's," Lena's familiar voice said.

I sighed in relief. "Hey, Lena, it's Sticks." Some band was warming up in the background, and the sound of their instruments came through the phone while I waited for her to respond.

"Wow, calling with an update so soon? You already famous?" She sounded so happy. I'd already forgotten we were going to fill her in on what happened after we played at The Palms. Dead bodies tended to cancel shows.

"Lena, we need some info," I said, keeping my voice as steady as possible. Tom and Sam crowded around the receiver, trying to listen as well.

"That's ominous." The clinking of glasses behind her punctuated her words. "What info do you need?"

"Charlie... He's been acting...off," I started, unsure how to tiptoe around that Charlie wouldn't be booking another gig. Ever.

"Sticks, you know Charlie's always got his fingers in too many pies." Her voice carried a note of caution that pricked my skin.

The payphone's receiver was sticky against my ear. I pulled it back so the others could hear. From the alley, the smells of motor oil and garbage combined with the sharp stench of fear coming off the three of us.

"Charlie's been pulling some side moves, meeting some people outside the club," I said, watching Tom out of the corner of my eye as he fiddled with the buttons and spikes on his sleeve.

"He's only been up here a few times with you guys," Lena said. "He always gives me the willies. He's slimy, you know? I've seen him with some people who weren't here for the bands or the drinks. No clue who they were, though."

Of course she didn't. My hopes fell a little. Lena always had her finger on the pulse. I had hoped she would have a little more for us.

"I figured you all knew what he was into. Sorry, I'm not being much help."

"I think there's a lot we don't know," I said, motioning to Sam's pocket, where she held the bag of powder we'd found. She nodded her head.

"Lena, one more thing." I imagined Lena leaning against the wall, cleaning a glass while she chatted with us, the Bakelite phone held up to her ear with her shoulder. The other band was still warming up behind her, some riffs coming through. They had a decent sound. "We found this baggy in Charlie's stuff. It's got a weird symbol on it. It's a snake eating its tail. Have you ever seen that before?"

There was a long pause, long enough that the lyrics from the band in the background were clear to me. Maybe they weren't that great after all.

"Sticks." She had caution edging into her words. "That symbol, it's bad news. I've seen it around. I found empty baggies of it in the bathrooms. You don't want to be involved with that shit. You don't need it."

"Fantastic," I huffed out, clenching my jaw—more dead ends.

Lena was an amazing bartender, but she kept her nose clean in every sense. She wasn't likely to have any more information about it.

"We'll stay out of it," I lied. "We don't want any trouble, and we didn't want Charlie in any either, but it sounds like he already is."

"It does," Lena agreed. "You three should be careful. It might be time for a new manager."

"You're not wrong about that," I said, my voice going flat. "Thanks for your help, Lena. We owe you one."

"Sure, Sticks, anytime."

I hung up the receiver and eyed Tom and Sam.

"I guess Charlie was playing a tune we knew nothing about." I pointed to the office door. "Let's go and find out if he was hiding anything else."

With a shared nod, we left the corner payphone behind and made our way to what used to be Charlie's sanctuary. His "fortress of solitude." He was a sucker for Superman movies. My breath was coming in short bursts, my pulse pounding. What was Charlie into? I couldn't help but feel we had just peeled back one layer of this mess to uncover three more.

I popped open the outside door, and we made our way up the creaky wooden stairs. The railing was rough on my palm. Fifty years of hands had worn off all the varnish. I grabbed the key under the fake potted plant outside the door marked "Charlie Fitzpatrick, Manager." I unlocked it and pushed it open, leading the way inside.

"You think we hit a dead end?" Tom asked from behind me as he closed the door.

"More like a torn-up map," I said, my stomach gnawing with tension. "Lena's seen the symbol before, which means it's all the way up in another country. This is way bigger than small-time Charlie and little old us."

"No one has been here," Sam said, shuffling through papers. "It's clean."

She was right. If they'd been after something Charlie kept here, the place would be turned upside down.

"Let's see what we can find," I said, opening the file cabinet. I spent about fifteen minutes going through it and the paperwork inside. I felt ridiculous, but I walked over and took down the pictures on the wall, thinking I would find a safe behind one of them. After finding nothing but the wall, I slumped down in Charlie's chair, dejected. This was the only place Charlie would have stashed stuff.

I opened the desk drawers and pulled them all out. A pencil tray slipped out of my hand from the top one, and several paperclips scattered across the inside.

"Shit," I cursed as I swept them into a pile. When I did, something shifted. I pressed down on the corner, and the paperclips spilled through the crack that had appeared on the false bottom.

"Guys!" I hissed. "Got something."

I gently lifted the panel. Sam and Tom gathered around me as I pulled it out and placed it beside me. A revolver was lying inside the drawer, glinting in the fluorescent light of the office. Right next to it was a bundle of cash. Stamped on the strip of paper holding the bundle together was a serpent eating its tail.

"Jesus," Tom whispered, slicing through the tension. "What the hell was Charlie into?"

"Nothing good," Sam concluded, stating the obvious.

"Should we?" Tom asked, pointing at the drawer.

"Touch nothing." Sam was all business as she said it. "Put everything back. We need to go."

We got everything back in order. Our minds raced as our hands did the same. In a few minutes, we had everything back the way it was and made our way out the door.

"Where to now?" Tom asked me. "Should we find Mick?"

"Deeper down the rabbit hole." I said, because where else would we go? "Before we go see Mick, we should find Spike. He'd be at the Underground by now. That's his usual haunt this time of day."

Spike, an older guy from the scene, was not the most dependable. He knew everyone, though. He was a regular at almost every venue, and I was sure he had a hefty tab at most of them. We'd known him for a couple of years. I wasn't sure we should trust him, but if anyone had inside information on how big this was, it was him.

The Underground—another dive in a sea of dives, but tonight, it held the promise of answers or the threat of more questions. Music thumping from inside, we pulled the van into a parking lot near the back. We made our way down the stairs to the subterranean venue, looking behind us the whole time.

As expected, Spike was propped up as close to the alcohol as possible. Head shaved bald, wearing an old letterman jacket covered in various homemade patches of multiple bands, slang, and curses.

"Hey, Spike," I called out as we approached, trying to make my voice carry over the music.

"Sticks," he greeted, then his eyes darted to Sam and Tom. "And all of Bombs Away. What's up, guys?"

"Got a minute?" I asked.

"Depends." He eyed us all. "Is the next round on you?"

I threw a fiver on the table. With it, I pulled from my pocket a piece of scrap paper where I'd copied the symbol from the baggie on the drive over.

"Have you seen this before?" I held it out for him to inspect as I said it.

Spike's eyes narrowed. I couldn't hear it with all the noise in here, but his chest puffed out like he sucked his breath in with surprise. His eyes went from squinting at the paper to wide at us as he registered what it was.

"Yeah," he said, hesitating. "I've seen it around. It's bad news. You don't want to be involved with that shit. Stick to this." He held up his almost empty rock glass and jingled the ice around.

"No choice, pal. We're in this already." I shrugged. "Where can I find more?"

"Where?" he asked, surprised. "Anywhere, man. Ask for some nose candy, and you'll find it. Most clubs in the nicer part of town have a guy or two supplying it."

"Thanks." I clapped him on the shoulder. "I appreciate it, Spike."

We all turned to make our way out.

"Bombs Away!" he called out as we got close to the exit. "You don't want to end up on these guys' Christmas list." He finished his drink. "Be careful."

I raised a two-fingered salute that said, "Will do," and walked out the back door.

Outside in the alley, the guitars and drums were muffled as the door closed behind us. It grew quieter as we made our way down the lane, then just a distant bass thump as we turned toward our ride home.

A shadow shifted. We stopped dead and backed against a dumpster pushed up alongside the building. The van sat battered and rusty as always, the back doors covered in bumper stickers.

The shadow moved again, checking the doors on both sides. Sam reached out and picked up a glass beer bottle from a nearby trash pile. She stepped forward. I held out my hand to hold her back, but she brushed it off.

As the shadow stepped out into the daylight to check the back door, Sam smashed the bottle against the corner of the dumpster.

The sound of a hundred tiny pieces of glass raining down in the alley broke the silence. The figure, no longer in shadow, glanced up, surprised. He was a young idiot of a kid, no more than fifteen, but he had tattoos already. I wasn't able to make out what they were, but he seemed young to have ink. He was likely looking to steal our ride or our gear still stowed away in the back.

We all emerged from our hiding spot. Sam was in the lead, standing tall. Tom with his giant mohawk, one fist held in his other hand. Me with my spikey black hair and a ratty Black Flag t-shirt. Not exactly the crew you wanted coming at you down a dark alley with a broken bottle.

The kid bolted. I imagined it like a cartoon; just a puff of smoke shaped like a dumbass was all that was left behind.

"Moron picked the wrong piece of shit to boost," Tom crowed with false bravado.

Sam tossed her bottle to the side as we made our way to our ride. I unlocked the sliding door and the passenger's side, then made my way around the front of the van. Unlocking the final door and opening it, I climbed behind the wheel.

Once we were settled, I asked, "I wonder what that was all about. After our gear?"

"Could be," Sam said, but I didn't think she was convinced.

"So what do we do now?" Tom piped up from the back.

"We need to go to some of the nicer clubs and start asking around. From what Spike said, it shouldn't be too hard."

"Yeah, at least we for sure don't look like cops," he said, arms spread wide to emphasize his outfit.

I laughed despite myself. With a practiced flick of the wrist, the engine sprang to life. The radio, loud but tinny, blasted out from the speakers.

"Let's turn over some rocks," I said. "There's gotta be something hiding under one of them."

With a lurch, we rolled forward out onto the street. I pushed the tape into the stereo, the songs becoming our soundtrack as we drove off. We were in way over our heads, but what choice did we have?

Chapter 5

Friday, September 5th, 1986, 8:32 p.m.

The van's engine rumbled and growled like a caged animal eager for release, the same restless energy coursing through us. Milwaukee streets flew by in a blur, and the three of us sat crammed into our rattling tin can while we plotted our next move. I had my mind on the redrawn snake symbol. It felt like it was burned into my retina. I couldn't forget it if I tried; I never would.

"Man, we gotta crack this," I muttered, my hands gripped the steering wheel tighter every moment. "It's like everyone knows more about this than we do. All this has been right here all along?"

Tom sat shotgun, picking at the holes in his jeans while he nodded in agreement. "Yeah, man. This symbol is all over. Here, up in Winnipeg, Charlie's office. How have we never seen it before?" Fear stained his voice, the kind that gnawed at you, keeping you up at night.

"Charlie was in deep," Sam said from the back, her voice slicing through the tension. She shifted forward, elbows on her knees, running her hand over her face. Her one visible eye was pale blue and locked onto mine when I glanced at the rearview again. "We find the thread. We pull."

"Damn straight," I said, swinging onto the next side street I found.

We pulled in and parked along the buildings within walking distance of a few downtown clubs. Our boots thumped along the sidewalk in time with each other, pounding out a rhythm like a war march. We made our way to the first place. As we approached, our clothes and hair were like camouflage. We blended in with the crowd waiting outside for the show tonight.

"Hey, got a sec?" I asked a couple of leather-clad punks leaning against the building a little way from the door.

One of them shrugged at me.

"Seen this before?" I said, holding up the sketch.

Their eyes scanned the paper, then each other and back to me.

"What's it worth to you?" the other one said with a sly grin.

"The satisfaction of helping someone out," Tom said, putting on his lead-singer swagger like a costume. "We're trying to help a friend of ours who's in a bad situation."

"If your friend is mixed up with that shit, you're right. It's bad," the first punk said. "All I know is, around a year ago, you didn't see this stuff. Then poof." He gestured with his hands like he was doing a magic trick. "It was everywhere."

"Thanks for the info," I said, the unease in my stomach solidifying into a lump.

Club after club, question after question, it was the same story. Almost everyone knew about the stuff. They'd seen it around or had a friend hooked on it. No one knew where it came from.

"We're chasing our tails," Tom groaned, the frustration cutting through his words.

"We keep pushing," said Sam, scanning the people around us. "Someone has to have more information."

As it got later, I grew less and less confident. Charlie's shadow loomed over us, a ghost of the man we'd known now stained with blood. The image of him lying there wouldn't get out of my head. He was smarmy and slippery, but he was our friend. He got us jobs when no one else would.

We were in too far to turn back now, though. So we pushed on and kept questioning, trying to memorize the lyrics to Charlie's final song.

"Let's keep moving," I said, leading the charge to the next bar or group of people we could pester with our questions. We would find something even if I had to ask every punk in Milwaukee.

Walking to the next place, we felt a buzz in the air that wasn't just from the neon glow flickering above our heads. This dive was a cesspool of leather and motorcy-cles—not our scene, but we had to try everything.

"Sticks, you sure about this?" Tom asked, his hair switching from blue to purple as the red neon blinked on and off.

"Do you have a better idea?" I asked though I knew he didn't. We were all running on fumes and desperation. I approached a group of bikers loitering outside. They were talking to each other but hadn't noticed us yet.

"Evening, fellas," I greeted.

All their eyes turned to me in an instant. I realized one was a large, muscled woman with close-cropped hair. *Shit...* Well, I was off to a great start. I cleared my throat and tried to get back on track. "I was wondering if I could ask you a question or two?"

They eyed us up and down, mouths agape, wondering what three punks were doing at "their" spot. After not getting a response, I continued, "Is anything strange hap-pening around here?" My question hung in the air for a moment, and I realized I was being too vague by trying to keep details out of it.

"Other than you three?" the largest in the group said, stepping forward.

"Something like this," I said, holding out the drawing. "We need more information. We're trying to help a friend who's in too deep."

"I'm sorry about your friend," he said, and I think he meant it. "If your friend is mixed up with that, it's too late. It would be best if you stopped sticking your nose where it doesn't belong. Anyone who goes looking for them isn't around much longer."

He turned back around to his friends.

"Another dead end," Tom muttered behind me as we walked away.

"We need to check by The Palms," I said, thinking aloud.

"No," Sam said, not an opinion. It was an order.

"Sam, listen," I pleaded with her. "I don't want to go back there either but to some places nearby. We'll lay low. I'm wondering if that's where Charlie was dealing…" I couldn't finish that sentence, so I started another. "That's where most of this stuff is, so the real answers should be there too. We'll go close and avoid passing by or going into The Palms. Deal?"

Sam's eyes had studied me the whole time I was speaking. "This is a bad idea," she said, but her shoulders slumped slightly. "We need to be quick about it and quiet." She turned back around and headed for the van without another word.

The section of town that held The Palms had a couple of other decent clubs. We made our way nearby, parked on a less-traveled side street, and walked the rest of the way. Staying inconspicuous was not easy for us. Six-foot blondes in leather and dudes with blue mohawks tended to stand out anywhere other than a punk show, but we did our best to keep to the shadows. The night was winding down, and we were running out of time.

The first place we went was a dead end. No one wanted to fess up to anything. The second was shaping up to be the same. We stopped by the bar and ordered a drink.

"Last call." The bartender was cleaning glasses nearby after he handed us our drinks. He was in his mid-to-late thirties, a little soft around the midsection but friendly enough.

"Question for you," I said.

"I'm all ears." He put his rag down and ambled over to us.

"Have you seen this before?" I said for the hundredth time tonight, putting the drawing in front of him.

His eyes flicked to it, the skin tightening around the corners, accentuating his crow's feet. "Yeah, I've seen it." He turned to go back to cleaning the glasses. Like everyone else, he didn't want to get involved.

"I understand," I said. "This is bad news. I wouldn't be asking if we weren't desperate. A friend of ours died over this. We need some help."

The bartender's face softened as he took the three of us in. Something shifted in his face; he'd made a decision. "I had a friend die recently, too. They think he was murdered."

The words struck me like a cymbal crash. Of course, word had gotten around about Charlie down here.

"I'm sorry about your friend," I said with genuine sympathy. The way his eyes swam when I spoke, he knew I meant it.

"Listen, this isn't some Scooby Doo cartoon. You three keep digging into this, and someone else will end up dead," he said, jabbing his finger onto the bar to drive his point home.

"We have to try," I said with determination.

"About a year ago, we had some new players move up from Chicago." He was quiet when he spoke now. "The head of this snake"—he tapped the drawing—"is barely a rumor. He's a tall guy, over six feet, all muscle. He has a bushy black beard you could scrub a pot with."

"Not even a name," I said. "You sure this isn't a Scooby Doo cartoon?" I was trying to make light of it.

"It's not funny, kid," he said, rubbing his nose with the back of his hand. He stuck his index finger at me, jabbing the air between us to drive his point home. "Watch yourself."

The conversation was over. He gathered the glasses and made his way into the back. At least we had something now.

"I don't know about you two, but I need some sleep." I yawned, and Sam nodded. Tom was dead on his feet. I didn't need him to say a word to know. "Let's head home and try again after we rest up a bit."

I wish we hadn't parked so far away, but you couldn't be too careful. We passed by some of the other clubs to get to where the van was. When we got about halfway back, our feet dragged along. Behind me, the sound of a shoe scuffing against concrete caught my attention. Someone was following us.

"Guys," I hissed, "we've got a tail."

Sam tensed next to me like a guitar string tuned way too high. She was about to turn when *click*.

The distinct sound of a gun's hammer being cocked back.

Sam froze. I froze. Tom let out a little whimper.

"You don't need to turn around," the gunman said, his voice dripping Chicago, sounding like one of the Blues Brothers. The hurried sounds of two other people joined the first. Now matched one per punk, they came to stand right behind us. "Sorry to put you in the dark, but this is how it's gotta be."

A rough cloth bag was pulled over my head, and the world went black.

Chapter 6

Saturday, September 6th, 1986, 12:06 a.m.

As the bag was ripped from my head, the brightness of the room blinded me. I blinked, trying to clear my vision. The world swam back into focus: a pool table, some fluorescent lights above it, and a rack on the wall with cues. I couldn't tell if it was a live band or recorded, but music was audible through the doorway. We had to be in the back room.

I swiveled my head around and saw the three that grabbed us. When my eyes went back to the pool table, two of the biggest goons I'd ever seen were in the middle of a game. That was the only word that summed them up—*goon*.

The two of them kept shooting pool, and we sat waiting. After a few minutes, the eight ball went into one of the corner pockets. They finally took notice of us. Both big, but both beardless.

"Rumor is you've been yapping at anyone who will listen about a symbol you found?" the biggest of the two asked. He had small, beady eyes and a nasty scar across his cheek.

"We're looking for information about our friend Charlie," I said, forcing my voice to remain even.

"Doesn't ring a bell," the smaller one said. He shifted his weight to lean on the pool cue he held as if it was the only thing keeping him upright.

"Cut the crap. Charlie Fitzpatrick, our manager. He bought drugs from you, and he wound up six feet under. Ring any bells now?"

The goon with the pool cue straightened up, his eyes narrowing to slits. "A lot of people buy drugs from a lot of different places," he hissed, his words cold. "If your friend got drugs somewhere and couldn't handle them, that's no business of ours. You three are sticking your noses where they don't belong. Stop asking questions."

His large friend cracked the knuckles on both hands like he was getting ready to beat a drum solo on my ribcage. The message was clear. Stop digging into this, or we would be next.

"I can't help it." Sarcasm dripped from my tone. "I'm a curious guy."

The humor was lost in the space between us. The threat hung in the air unspoken, as dark as the tattoos across their forearms—snakes eating their tails.

"Last warning," Pool Cue said, and something in his stance told me he meant it. "Walk away if you know what's good for you."

I wanted to ask more, but whatever response I got wouldn't help anyone if I was dead. Charlie deserved better than what he got. I was going to make damn sure he at least got justice, but staring down the barrel of whatever these guys had in store would put an end to all that real quick.

"Come on," I muttered, signaling to Tom and Sam, standing up and backing away from the goons without breaking eye contact. "Let's bounce before we end up part of the scenery."

"Not so fast," Pool Cue said as the black bags dropped back over our eyes.

We were shuffled back into a vehicle and driven for a few minutes to where they had snatched us. Ripping the bags off our heads, they shoved us out of the still rolling vehicle. We tumbled over each other and slammed to a stop against the sidewalk, our arms and legs covered in all manner of cuts and bruises.

"I think I pissed myself," Tom said. I couldn't tell if he was joking or not.

"They were all talk," I tried to reassure him.

His eyes were wild, darting around. He cringed like shadows would jump out of every dark corner to grab us.

"All talk and a *gun*!" he squeaked. "What the hell was Charlie into?"

"I have no idea. All we have are pieces. We need the rest of the puzzle," I said, dejected.

"We need evidence," Sam said, her pale blue eyes scanned the dark street, her brows furrowed while the wheels turned in her mind, trying to put it together. "Real evidence. Something that leads to their boss."

"Right," Tom said. "If we can find anyone who's not too scared to talk."

"Let's go home," I suggested, arching my back and stretching my sore muscles. "We all need some sleep."

We headed back to the secluded side street we had parked on. Somewhere in this city was the proof we needed. Something to use as leverage to prove our innocence. I hoped I lived long enough to find out what it was.

Chapter 7

Saturday, September 6th, 1986, 1:07 a.m.

"**M**an, that was too close," Tom gasped out. He was tugging at his sleeve, eyes scanning every corner for some hidden threat.

"We've got this, man. We're almost home," I said.

We pulled up to the back of our place and locked the van up tight, checking every door twice. We made our way down to the entrance of our flat with the most important of our equipment. I had an amp in each hand, Sam had her bass, and Tom had his guitar.

We rounded the final corner to see a figure standing by the front door, illuminated by the overhead light. I moved in front of the group to stand between the figure and my friends. Sam grabbed my shoulder from behind to warn me right before someone called out to us.

"Francis Marshall?"

I squinted into the brightness, my eyes trying to adjust. I saw a suit, a tie, a badge in their hand.

"Who's asking?" though I was pretty sure I already knew the answer.

"Your name is Francis?" Tom whispered behind me.

"Not the time, Tom," I hissed.

"I'm Detective Harris," the figure said, holding his badge out a little further. "Mind if I have a word? Have you seen your manager lately?"

"Charlie?" Tom said, his Adam's apple bobbing like he'd swallowed something that wasn't agreeing with him. I knew this was coming. I had hoped we would get more time.

"I can't say we have," I answered, cutting Tom off before he let something slip that we couldn't take back. "Why? Is something wrong?"

Harris's expression didn't change, but the weight of his stare was on me, all of us, looking for cracks in our story. Sam remained a statue, her face unreadable.

"Let's just say that he's not answering his phone," Harris said, the way he looked at me suggesting an accusation. Maybe that was my imagination running wild.

"I'm sorry," I replied, keeping my voice as steady as possible. A lump formed in my throat, my palms slick with sweat. "The last time we saw Charlie was before we hit the road to Winnipeg. We called before we came home and checked in, and we told him we'd see him later."

Harris narrowed his eyes, all skepticism. He tapped his shoe against the concrete like a metronome. "Strange," Harris said with a calm voice, but it had an edge like a razor. "A manager who's always on top of things, all of a sudden isn't checking in. No next gig? You three don't seem all that concerned."

"We have been worried. We asked around. No one has seen him. We went to his office, and no one answered." I tried to inject some truth into my lie. I'd read somewhere that helped. I set the amps down and shoved my sweaty hands into my pockets, trying to hide the signs of my insecurity. "What do you want from us? We're a band. We bang on drums and strum guitars. We don't solve mysteries."

"Maybe so." He took a step closer to me, standing up to his full height. He was shorter than Sam, but still towered over me. "You're not telling me something. Where did you go after the show?"

"We came straight home and slept," I said, my mind trying to separate fact from fiction. "When we got up, we tried Charlie at his office, but he didn't answer. We stopped by, and no one was there. We asked around town a little, went to a few bars, and came back here.

"Nobody split off? Took a detour?" His questions came sharp and fast.

"No detours." I kept my gaze on him, a staring contest. *Winner takes all.* "We stick together all the time."

"It's sweet you're all so chummy." Harris leaned in closer. "Your van was seen all over town, even at some places known to be criminal hotspots."

"We were trying to drum up our next job." The lies were coming easier now. "Charlie hadn't booked us, so we drove around to find a place to play at the last minute. We gotta eat. We've got bills to pay."

"You weren't looking for work with Big Tony?" Harris said, one hand resting on his revolver, the other reaching up to run over the almost bald pate of his head.

"Who's Big Tony?" I said, but I had a sneaking suspicion it was who we were looking for all along.

Harris had given us the one thing we needed—a name.

The detective let out a long sigh. We had witnessed him make his move. He'd wanted more of a reaction or a confession. The problem was that we were as clueless as we seemed. Harris rubbed his hand over his face. His eyes alternated between Tom and Sam.

"Tom. Thomas Williams. Anything you'd like to add?" Harris stepped closer to Tom, invading his personal space. He looked down his nose, waiting for a response.

"N-nothing," Tom stammered, and for a second, I was sure he was about to crack. Tom didn't have the best track record when it came to being brave. The thing was, Tom was a punk through and through, and he hated authority. His dad was a cop, and from the stories I'd been told, they didn't have the best relationship. Tom was biting his lip hard enough to draw blood. "Will you call us if you find out anything about Charlie? We're worried about him. Do you have any leads?"

The silence hung in the air. I realized Tom deserved more credit than I gave him. He came through when we needed him.

Harris paused. "We're working all the angles. I'm not at liberty to discuss specifics in an active investigation." He wasn't budging on this. "What about you?" He pointed a finger at Sam. "You've been quiet. Do you have anything to add?"

Sam stared him dead in the eyes. "Nope."

Harris blew out a sharp breath. "Do you three think this is a game? This investigation is ongoing. I need the three of you to stay in town. I'll be back. Count on it."

The detective spun on his heel and stormed away.

The realization of everything crashed down on us. We'd lied to the police, and they'd be back—probably to arrest us, but we got some information, too.

"Big Tony," I whispered. "That has to be the guy, right?"

"It's likely," Sam answered, her eyes watching Harris get into his car and drive away. "We need to be careful."

"Does anyone else feel like that cop knew a whole lot more than he was letting on?" Tom said, voice shaking from the encounter. He'd been brave, but that was wearing off. "We gotta get to the bottom of this."

"We need to hide the van off the street," Sam suggested. "They've been able to track us."

She was right. I hadn't even thought of it until Harris let slip that they'd seen it all over town.

Sam reached out her hand to me. "Give me the keys. I'll bring it inside one of the garage bays."

I handed them over and watched her disappear back to where we'd parked. Tom and I started unloading our equipment into the storage closet. He had a stern face, his brow furrowed.

"You alright, man?"

"Yeah," he responded, then continued after a second thought. "You know what? No, I'm nowhere close to alright."

"Tom," I tried to say, but he held up his hand to stop me.

"No, man. What are we doing? I mean, I don't like cops, but we're lying to them. That dude will be coming back to arrest us. What are we going to do? We've got a name. That's awesome. What the hell are we supposed to do now?" Tom sucked in some air after his tirade, then sighed, slumping against the wall. "We're screwed, man."

"We gotta keep digging. We're going to find something soon." I almost believed myself when I said it. "Big Tony has to be involved somehow. I bet Charlie owed him money or something."

Tom didn't say a word. He was done; he didn't want to play this game. We were caught in a trap, and I was gnawing at my leg to break free. I wanted to avoid ending up as some terrible headline in tomorrow's paper.

A few minutes later, a screech of rusted metal echoed through the building. Sam was wrenching open the rolling metal door on the far side. Headlights lit up the interior of the building as the van rumbled in through the door.

The engine cut off, and Sam hopped out, slamming the door behind her. There was more screeching as she pulled the door back down and made sure it was locked tight. She stopped at the other three and tested the locks at each one. She jogged over to us when she was finished.

"All set. No police or thugs around." Sam was trying to wipe off the orange rust from the doors but wasn't having much luck. "We're all set. You'd need a blowtorch to break in."

"We..." Tom cleared his throat. "We need to find something already. None of Tony's goons will give us anything. We're no closer to finding the actual dude, which I don't even think we should do. Oh, and now the police are snooping around. Telling us not to leave town? They're going to arrest us." Tom's eyes darted to Sam, trying desperately to find someone to agree with him since I wasn't going to budge.

"We need to keep going," I said, knowing it wasn't what he wanted to hear. "We're close. I know it. We need to find Big Tony and see if he has blood on his hands."

"How do you know he won't kill us the minute he gets the chance?" Tom's voice inched up in pitch and volume. "Whoever killed Charlie isn't going to mind killing us either."

Sam nodded along while he talked. "Tom's right," she said once he had finished.

"Thank you!" Tom blurted out. "At least one person is making sense."

"Sticks is right, too. We need to keep investigating this," Sam said, her eyes turning to Tom. Her face softened a little. "We've been reckless; we need to be more careful."

Tom sighed, hanging his head, knowing we wouldn't give up. "Yeah, *careful* would be a plus."

My mind was racing with ideas and all the information we'd gathered, and it didn't amount to much. Everything still led to Big Tony. We had to get to a safe place to hide out so we could figure out our next move.

"We need to go see Mick," I said. "We haven't talked with him yet. He might let us crash at his place, and we can see if he has any info about Charlie."

"We're not staying here?" Tom tried his best not to stare longingly up the stairs towards his bed.

"We *can't* stay here." Sam was already striding towards the door.

"Oh, man, this sucks," Tom muttered half under his breath.

"We're all tired, but this is the first place that the detective is coming back to," I said, placing my hand on Tom's shoulder. "I'd rather not be here when the cavalry shows up."

Tom nodded, agreeing without saying a word. Sam was already walking. It would take us a while to make our way there without wheels.

Like a scene in *Night of the Living Dead*, we shambled along. Twenty-four hours with almost no sleep would do that to you. Harris was on top of this case; he would have a list of known associates for us. We couldn't stay with Mick long. One night at the most, and we'd need to move somewhere more secure. We needed a moment to rest, a moment to think. Since we got back from Winnipeg it had been one thing after another. We were close; I could feel it. Mick would help us out, and we could start fresh after a bit of sleep.

Chapter 8

Saturday, September 6th, 1986, 3:07 a.m.

About forty minutes later, we rounded the corner to Mick's building, a downtown high-rise. Mick always seemed to be doing well for himself. His band had broken up almost a year ago, right as we were coming on the scene. He was always around, though, helping other musicians and slotting in on guitar here and there where it was needed. He was also always ready to party.

We thanked the rock gods as we entered the building. There was an elevator. I didn't think we could have made it up the stairs at that point. After the elevator dinged its arrival, we piled in, and Tom punched the button for the seventh floor.

Muzak dug itself into our heads as we rose in the elevator. I wanted to plug my ears, but I didn't have the energy. The elevator dinged again, announcing our arrival on the seventh floor. The doors slid open, and we shuffled down the hallway, stopping halfway to knock on Mick's door.

The minute it opened, the stench of stale cigarettes and beer greeted us. I was slumped against the doorframe. Tom was swaying in place. The only thing standing up straight was his hair. Sam acted like she was bored, but if you paid close attention, there were also signs of weariness around her eyes.

"Jesus, what the hell happened to you three?" Mick asked with a wry smile on his face. "You look like a warmed-up turd."

"We feel like it too." I couldn't help but smile back. "Can we crash here? It's been a hell of a couple of days."

"Yeah, come on in. I'll grab some beers." Mick stepped into the apartment, leaving the door open for us to enter.

"Thanks, Mick. We owe you one," Tom said as he slumped down onto the couch, his head lying back, his eyes already shut.

The apartment was ritzy, like the lifestyles of the rich and famous. It had new furniture and a view of the city. Besides the lingering odor of cigarettes, it was a flawless model home. I always figured Mick came from money; his apartment proved it to me.

I remembered a year or so ago when we'd met him. Charlie had just started repping us. We were beyond excited to have a manager. Finding gigs without one was not going well for us. Mick helped set up a few of our first shows. Charlie had worked with his band before us. No one ever talked about why they broke up, only that

Mick was the only one who had stayed in town in the aftermath.

"Tres cervezas," Mick said as he came around the corner from the kitchen, juggling the beers. He saw Tom passed out and gently placed his down on the table in front of him. He handed us our beers and slumped in the chair beside the couch. "Sit down. You look like you're about to fall over."

You didn't have to tell us twice. Sam and I each sat on a section of the couch, trying not to disturb Tom.

"We appreciate this," I said.

"Don't mention it, I never sleep anyway." Mick waved a dismissive hand. "I'm happy to see you all again.

Mick downed his beer all at once and set it down beside him. He scooted to the edge of his seat to get closer to us. "What's going on? What kind of trouble are you in?" He glanced between us, trying to get a read on what was happening.

"You ever see this before?" I threw the folded paper over to him.

He snagged it out of the air and unfolded it. He studied the drawing on it, and his eyes widened in surprise. "I've seen this around and it's bad news. We're talking cocaine, gangsters, the whole deal. I didn't think you messed with this scene."

"We don't, and we never will. You know we're about the music." He nodded while I said it. Bombs Away kept their noses clean.

"If you're not involved in this," he said, looking up from the image of the snake eating its tail, "then what are you doing with it?"

"Charlie's dead," Sam said. I guessed she was done being coy about it.

"Oh, shit," Mick said, his body tensing up. He sucked in a sharp breath. "Who do you think did it? Where? When did this happen?"

He was upset, almost frantic, with eyes darting between all of us. He and Charlie weren't close after he stopped managing their band. They never spoke when they were in the same room together. I figured there was bad blood after his band broke up. His reaction was telling me he must have still held some interest somewhere for Charlie's well-being, even if he'd pushed it down for a while.

"Someone is trying to make people think it was me." I pulled my drumsticks out of my back pocket. "We went to meet him for rehearsal and found him lying there with one of my sticks jammed in his eye. We cut and ran. We've been trying to figure all this out ever since."

Mick whistled and shook his head. "Who did it?"

"What do you know about Big Tony?" I asked.

"If you know that name, you're in deep shit; deeper than you realize," Mick said, folding the paper back up. "This is his symbol." He held the paper up in the air before tossing it to me. "It's the reason my band broke up."

"I had no idea. I'm sorry," I said to Mick, grabbing the paper as it slid across the coffee table.

"We kept it on the down low when our bassist Steve got hooked. It was a downward spiral. It only took a month or two, and everything fell apart. We went our separate ways from Charlie, and here we are. That was right when this stuff was coming on the scene. Right before you all started out. The name Big Tony was floating around some of the bigger clubs. But after a while, people stopped saying his name like he's the bogeyman. It seemed like an ignore-the-problem-and-pretend-it-doesn't-exist situation."

"Sam found a baggie on Charlie with the symbol," I told him. "We think Tony has something to do with it. We don't have all the answers yet, but it's what we have to go on."

"He's a ghost. No one's seen him; if they have, they're not talking. He has runners do everything for him." Mick lay back in his chair. "You should split. Get the hell out of here. Let the cops deal with this and disappear."

"They already paid us a visit. That's why we're here," Sam said, shrugging. "We couldn't stay at home."

"Well, like I said, you can crash here. We can try to come up with a plan," Mick said, getting up from his chair and heading back to the kitchen. "You want another one?"

I glanced at Sam. She shook her head. She hadn't touched the one she had, and neither had I. "Nah, we're fine," I called out.

Mick came back in and sat down, draining another beer along the way. "I doubt Big Tony would kill Charlie himself." He sank back into his chair, eyes on the ceiling. "He'd send someone to do it."

"But why Charlie to begin with?" I asked. "I never saw Charlie with drugs before. Did you?"

"Charlie got up to some stuff back in the day," Mick noted, a sly, almost imperceptible smirk playing on his lips. "He was probably into Big Tony for some money."

Something was nagging at me. I didn't know what, but it was an instinctual thing down in the pit of my stomach. A sixth sense telling me we'd said too much. Sam shifted forward on the couch. She looked like she was ready to run for the door. She must have felt it as well.

"I'm sorry to drag you into this, Mick." I said, "We should go. I don't want to bring any trouble to your doorstep."

"Don't worry about it," Mick said, waving a hand. "You should rest while you can, then jet out of here. If anyone shows up, I'll throw them off your tail."

He smiled easily, and the unease receded a bit. Mick was a friend. I was tired, that was all. I needed to get some sleep and put the day behind me.

"Did you drive here?" he asked. "I always liked that van you all have."

"Nah, we walked," I said, leaning back on the couch.

"No wonder you look like crap. You're over in the warehouse district, right? That's miles from here."

"Yeah, it sucked," I said, closing my eyes for a second. I forced them open again, picking my head up. If I let them close, I was going to be out cold. "You know a bit about this stuff, right. You think you could introduce us to someone who can take us to Big Tony himself?"

"That's a tall order." He threaded his hands together, "I'm not connected or anything, but I don't think you can waltz in and talk to the boss. You gotta have something to offer."

"We don't have anything," I said, clueless.

"Maybe I can do something," Mick said. "I might have someone I can reach out to; they can at least point you in the right direction."

"We'd appreciate it. His goons already threatened us once. I don't need a repeat of that."

"What?" Mick shot up in his chair. "You got grabbed?"

"Yeah, we were checking around all the clubs, and they grabbed us off the street."

"Jesus, you all need to be more careful." He was up, heading into the kitchen for another beer. I wondered how many he had in there. "You can't go throwing that picture around. You're lucky you don't have a cop face. You would have been dead already."

He was right. We hadn't been careful at all. Driving all over the place, talking to anyone and everyone, not knowing who was behind it all. It was dumb luck that we weren't dead or arrested yet.

Mick came back in, draining his next beer. "First things first," he said after he slugged it back. "You three need some sleep. I'll make some calls and see what I can dig up."

"We appreciate it, Mick, really. I can't thank you enough."

"Don't thank me yet," he said with a shrug.

Sam and I settled back into the couch. I closed my eyes, and I was out before my head was all the way down.

It wasn't a restful sleep. The last twenty-four hours of events kept flashing through my dream. Charlie dead. My drumstick covered in blood. Detective Harris chasing me, calling out, "I know you did this. This is all your fault!"

I shoved through a door in my dreams, and I was right back looking at Charlie's body again.

I turned and ran back through the door, right into the hands of the goons. Pool Cue staring at me and tapping the cue on the ground. He swung it at my head. I flinched and was in an empty room, a shadow standing above me.

"You was trying to find me?" the shadow said with a thick Chicago accent. "You shouldn't do that. It's bad for your health." A huge ghostly hand slammed down on me, turning into billowing black smoke.

I was behind my drum set, looking out at the crowd. We were performing at The Palms. The audience was full of people. Lights flashed over them, and I could see that everyone had Charlie's face. Each one had a drumstick coming out of their eye, blood trickling out like tears. Tom was singing, "Why didn't we save him?"

I jerked awake on the couch. The lights in the room were all off, and I could see it was still dark outside through the windows. Just the faintest hint of pre-dawn light on the horizon.

Sam was sitting upright next to me. She held a finger to her lips. I froze and could hear Mick on the phone in the next room. His voice was almost a whisper, but I made out what he was saying.

"I don't know where the van is. I've got them, though. They're right here."

I gaped at Sam.

"We gotta go," she mouthed. "*Now.*"

I put a hand over Tom's mouth and shook him. He woke up struggling. I held my finger to my lips and motioned to the door. His eyes flicked around the room, trying to find his bearings.

We made our way to the door one careful step at a time, each one deliberate and tentative as it tested for a squeak before moving on.

Mick's voice still reached us from the next room. "What do I want? Now that Charlie's gone, I want back in."

Sam, making no sound at all, reached the door first. Grabbing Mick's keys off the hook, she carefully turned the deadbolt and started to open it. It creaked, the hinges protesting the sudden movement.

Shit.

We ran for the elevator like the devil himself was behind us. I could hear Mick cursing into the handset as we bolted out.

Fate was on our side at least, the elevator was still on this floor. It slid open easily so the three of us could rush inside. I hit the button for the bottom level. The doors closed just as I saw the one to Mick's apartment start to crack open again. I was glad there was only one elevator here.

Muzak surrounded us again while we waited to bolt out the door at the bottom. I didn't recognize the song, but it was terrible.

Chapter 9

Saturday, September 6th, 1986, 5:13 a.m.

"T raitor," Sam spat out as we ran, her voice seething with rage.

"Toss me the keys," I said, holding out my hand to her. I caught them as she threw them over. The parking lot was dimly lit by streetlights placed too far apart. I searched around for Mick's car.

"Delta-88!" Tom barked out, inclining his head to the beast of a car. More of a boat than a land vehicle, pale yellow and trying its best to be a Cadillac, but not quite pulling it off.

"Let's go, let's go!" I yelled as we dashed for it, all piling in as soon as I unlocked the doors. We sank into the couch-like seats, which stank of stale cigarettes and fake pine deodorizer.

I turned the key, and it started with a powerful rumble. We squealed out of the parking lot as Mick came out the door, but he didn't follow us. I wondered what game he was playing.

"What the hell is going on?" Tom called from the back seat. "What happened? I thought Mick was helping us."

"He sold us out while we were sleeping," Sam snapped.

"What? No way." Desperation was in Tom's voice and his eyes. He stared behind us at Mick's fading figure, standing in the doorway, watching us go. "Why would he do that?"

I cranked the wheel and turned the car to the right at the first intersection. "Believe it, loud and clear. He said, 'I have them. I want back in.'"

"Everyone's against us." Tom slumped back in the seat. "What are we going to do?"

"Right now, we're going to get as far away from him as possible." I floored the gas and sped down the city street.

The Delta-88 surged forward, the engine rumbling and vibrating the car around us. In the mirrors, I only saw empty streets behind us. That didn't mean anything, though. Mick would have been able to catch us if he'd come right after us. He stayed on the phone. They knew we were on the run.

"Man, I never thought I'd be on the lam in Mick's old banana boat," Tom muttered, trying to find some humor in the chaos.

"We're not in the clear yet." I said, my knuckles going white as I gripped the steering wheel tighter.

Headlights bloomed behind us as a car turned onto the road. Sam spun around in the passenger seat, squinting at the car in the distance. She must have been able to make it out as it passed under a streetlight.

"Black Caddy, coming up fast." She whirled back around in her seat.

"You think it's Big Tony's crew? How could they find us?" I asked, hoping for some reassurance. It didn't come.

"You can't hide a gigantic yellow monster on wheels!" Tom screeched, his hands gripping the headrests.

"They're right on us. Go!" Sam urged.

I pushed the pedal to the floor, and we accelerated into the approaching dawn.

"East side, Sticks! Head for the bridge!" Tom directed, leaning over the front seat.

I nodded, swerving hard to the right. The car was enormous; it was like driving a tank. It fishtailed around the corner, the back end taking out a trash can. Papers and other garbage flew into the air in our wake.

Sam's eyes narrowed on the road in front of us, watching for anything that might jump in our way. I scanned the mirrors again. My hands trembled, dread consuming me. Mick had betrayed us. Was there anyone on our side?

The Delta-88's engine thundered as I gave it more gas. We shot across the bridge and back between the buildings on the other side. The Caddy still followed behind us, two pinpricks of light growing larger. We weren't losing them; they were gaining on us.

"Punch it!" Tom yelled. "They're right on us!" His mohawk silhouetted in the bright light now flooding the car.

"Already on it!" My eyes fixed on the road that unwound like a cable before us.

As we tore through downtown Milwaukee, the city was a frenzied blur of streetlights and shadows. The speedometer climbed higher, and I felt the car strain as we pushed its limits, every twist and turn demanding all my focus.

"Keep it steady." Sam's voice cut through the engine noise, her accent thicker with tension. "We can't afford to tailspin."

"Spinning out is the least of our worries if they catch up." I ground my teeth together, feeling the weight of the responsibility pressing down on me. I had to lose them, and fast. I exchanged glances with Sam, each willing the other to see any signs of danger. Tom's short, panicked breaths from the back had me worried about him. "Tom, how are we looking?"

"They're still gaining on us," Tom replied, an octave higher than usual.

"It's not about speed," Sam said, her voice full of urgency. "It's about being unpredictable."

"Right," I said, forcing a smirk. "Time to get creative then."

We were outsiders, punks, rebels. We were used to fighting the system and standing up for ourselves. This was different, the stakes were life or death. Our only weapon was a whale of an Oldsmobile that took corners in slow motion.

"Why the hell does Mick have such terrible taste in cars?" I punched my fist against the wheel in a vain effort to coax some more speed out of the beast.

"Next time we steal a car," Tom said, "I'm choosing."

"Deal!" I agreed, fishtailing around another corner at the last moment. I kept checking the rearview, wishing to see something different. There was only darkness behind us for a moment.

The gut-punch glow of headlights flooded the Delta's review mirror as the Caddy rounded the corner. My pulse kicked up to a beat I would have struggled to keep up with.

"Damn it!" Sam spat from beside me, her fist smacking against the dash. "Can't this heap go any faster?"

"Doing everything I can over here!" I yelled back.

The engine rumbled beneath us. Fear spiked through every nerve, but beneath it was determination. The kind you found when you stepped out in front of a packed venue and struck your first chord. No turning back.

I ducked and weaved the Delta-88 through morning traffic, slipping between cars like a needle in a groove. Horns blared their disapproval, but I didn't care. I urged the car forward, trying my best to erase those damn headlights behind us.

"Watch it!" Tom shouted as I narrowly missed clipping a taxi that had decided to start a game of chicken with us.

"I didn't see him," I lied. The truth was, I was exhausted, and I didn't react fast enough. This needed to be over. Flashes of middle fingers from other drivers, the shocked faces of pedestrians as they jumped back onto the curbs and out of our way—that was all I was seeing.

I swerved and barely missed another car. The Delta rocked on its axles in protest.

"Sticks, man, you're gonna kill us all!" Tom warned, the words half lost in the ruckus of the chase, his hands gripping the "oh-shit" handle above the window.

"I'm going to have to get in line," I quipped back. Gallows humor was the only thing I was able to muster.

I shook myself awake. This wasn't a chase. The stakes were higher than that. This was a full-throttle sprint for answers and justice for Charlie. I couldn't let anything stop us, not even that metallic monster behind us.

"Left!"

Tom's shout snapped me back to reality. His finger pointing ahead of us shot into the front seat. "Up ahead! Turn left!"

"Got it," I growled back, my hands gripping the wheel tighter. With the way this beast cornered, it was going to be tricky. "Stay frosty," I said, cranking the wheel hard to the right.

"You sure?" Sam's voice was tight with anxiety beside me.

"Trust me," I insisted. *Sure* wasn't a word in my vocabulary at this moment.

The Delta's tires screeched in protest as we lined up with the mouth of the alley, a sliver of hope. All we had to do was squeeze through. The engine thrummed as I floored it, sounding far more confident than me.

We shot between the buildings, sparks flying as the side mirrors clipped off. Any slight movement to either side was met with more sparks, the car's bodywork singing a symphony of scrapes and crunches against the walls. It held, though. We shot out the other side and back onto the streets.

"Follow that!" I exclaimed to the mystery driver of the Caddy. We all sighed in relief. There was no way they would be able to get through there.

Headlights bloomed in the mirrors as they easily turned onto the road behind us. They knew this part of town far better.

"Shit!" I said, cursing the Cadillac and whatever goons were stuffed inside it.

It was clear the Caddy had been toying with us all along. They sped up onto our tail, their lights filling the back window. The Cadillac's engine grew louder as they smashed into us. Our back end swung around and up onto the sidewalk out of control.

I cranked the wheel, trying to get the car back on the road, but it was too late. The back bumper collided with a fire hydrant, sending a spray of water into the sky. I turned hard to the right and was able to straighten it out. I stomped on the gas and heard a loud pop. I figured the car must have backfired. We probably knocked something loose.

Two more quick pops and the back window shattered, showering Tom with glass.

"What the hell!" he shouted, dropping into a crouch in the back seat. "They're shooting at us!"

I whipped the car hard to the right onto the next street to break their line of sight. Then, a hard left, another right. I zigged and zagged through the city, doing my best not to let them have a straight shot at us again.

"Lights!" Sam barked out.

I reached down and turned the knob towards me. Everything went dark outside as well as on the dash. I kept making erratic turns, trying my best to stay a step ahead. I didn't see anything behind me, but no way in hell was I stopping yet. I sped forward down a straightaway and turned down a narrow lane between two buildings about three or four stories in height.

The lane led to a small parking lot wedged in between four buildings. I screeched the car to a stop and killed the engine. It died with a shudder, falling silent. We didn't waste a heartbeat. Our doors flew open like the gates of hell themselves as we spilled out onto the asphalt.

"There." Sam pointed to a fire escape ladder.

"Go, go, go!" I said, my voice more of a growl than a command.

The ladder was salvation in cold steel. My hands clamped onto the rungs with a grip that would leave bruises. Up we went, a frantic tangle of denim and leather. Sam was right behind me, her arms flexing as she hoisted herself up, gaining on me and pushing me to go faster. I caught a glimpse of her face—determination, and a hint of fear. That made me get moving. If Sam was scared, I wasn't about to take my time.

Metal clanged and rattled under our weight, the fire escape groaning in protest. My lungs burned, each breath a fiery gulp of air that tasted of rust and desperation.

We hit the rooftop with hearts pounding double-time. I hauled myself over the edge, rolling onto the gravel-covered surface. Sam followed right behind, a blond comet streaking through the night. Tom was last, eyes crazed with fear. He put his back to the wall, gasping for air that felt too thick to breathe.

"Made it," Tom wheezed out, but the victory was short-lived.

We heard the screeching brakes from the main road. They must have spotted us somehow. Below, the Cadillac came into view. Headlights flooded the area, illuminating the Delta.

We all sucked in our breath and held it. Four buildings, four ways in and out. We hoped they would have no idea which way we ran.

I peeked over the side again, seeing the skid marks that had drawn a line right into the alley we had escaped to. I cursed the Delta for giving us away, the Benedict Arnold of Oldsmobiles.

Two goons clambered out of the Caddy, eyes wild with thwarted rage, mouths spewing curses. They checked each alley, returned to the Caddy, and sped off into the night.

"That was close," I muttered, pulling back from the edge. "We got lucky."

"Are they gone?" Tom squeaked out, not daring to peek over the ledge himself.

"Like rats down a sewer pipe," Sam answered, breath forming clouds that floated away into the dim light.

We huddled together, half expecting the Caddy to reappear like some bad dream you couldn't shake.

But the morning remained still—no roars of an engine, no headlights hunting us. Only the distant sound of a police siren, probably chasing down some other poor bastards.

With our backs pressed against the wall, we watched the sun slowly rising. We shivered and stayed close to each other for warmth. I had no idea how much time passed but realized I was taking quick, shallow breaths. My body was expecting those goons to come clambering up the fire escape at any moment, guns blazing.

"I think we shook 'em," Tom chattered through his shivering.

The tension left us for a moment, and I laughed, a rough, jagged thing that scraped its way up from my gut. We were alive, against all odds, and that seemed like a victory.

"Charlie would have been proud," I said, my voice thick with memories of him telling us to "stick together, and you'll go places!" The slicked-back hair, the shiny, cheap suits.

"Let's get to the bottom of this," I said to Sam and Tom. To myself, I was thinking, *Before we all wind up dead, too.*

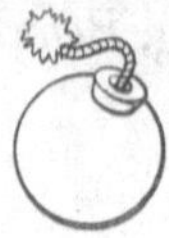

Chapter 10

Saturday, September 6th, 1986, 7:26 a.m.

A couple of hours had passed since the goons left discouraged, but we couldn't bring ourselves to leave the roof. Tom kept pacing to get warm. Sam sat quietly, lost in her thoughts. Still, like the cold couldn't touch her.

I sat with my back pressed against the bricks, my head tipped up, and my vision filled with a bright blue sky. My hands pulled at the frayed edges of my t-shirt. When was the last time I'd changed this? What day was it today?

Tom cleared his throat. "So Mick is involved with Big Tony somehow?" His frustration matched my own. "But how? Why?" His hands smoothed his mohawk, a nervous tic he'd developed over the years.

"Mick liked the track, right?" I asked. "Is it possible he blew all his money on horses and got in debt with the wrong people?"

"Doesn't explain the drugs," Sam reasoned. "And how does that link to Charlie? He didn't gamble."

"You're right," I said. "It doesn't make sense. We didn't know Charlie was into that scene. I figured Mick was, but not this deep."

I stood up on the roof and paced with frantic energy. I needed to move, to do something. That and if I didn't get some blood flowing, I would freeze solid.

"What's the connection between the three of them?" My feet scuffed along the roof as I walked, tiny rocks skittering in every direction with each step. "Charlie had to be a pawn. They were using him somehow. Mick said he wanted back in, so he was out for some reason."

"Damn it!" Tom exclaimed. Sam and I turned to him while he ranted. "This is like trying to piece a jigsaw puzzle together with half the pieces missing. We don't know shit."

"We're looking at this from the wrong perspective," Sam suggested, her brow furrowed in thought. "We need to stop thinking about the people. They want something."

"Like what?" Tom asked, his voice irritated.

"The van!" I recalled. "Mick was talking about the van to whoever he was on the phone with."

"Why the hell would someone want our shitty van?" Tom chimed in.

"Something in it? Something that Charlie had that they wanted?" At least this was a start, a next step.

"Well, we can't stay up here forever," Sam said, making her way over to the fire escape.

"What could be in the van that they're after?" Tom wondered. "It's all guitar cables and empty beer cans."

"Charlie must have seen something he shouldn't have." I was channeling the old black-and-white movies I watched with my grandfather, the ones where the lead character called every guy a "chum" and every girl a "doll. "He might have hidden some evidence in there—a recording or some paperwork?"

We were walking a thin line, teetering between danger and discovery. Whatever secrets our van held, they better be worth the risk we were taking. I inhaled deeply and steeled myself for what came next.

"Okay, we head back to the one place we shouldn't go." I turned to my bandmates. "Home."

"This is a bad idea," Tom said, ever the optimist.

We descended the fire escape in a cloud of rust and resignation. Detective Harris had to be looking for us by now, and the goons were after us and our van. So, what would Bombs Away do? Leave town? Start over? No, we headed right to where they were all waiting for us.

"Okay," I started as we walked out of the side street, "we need to make this quick. We swing in, check the van, and then get the hell out. No messing around."

"Agreed," Sam said.

Tom nodded, his mouth a thin line that said, "I didn't sign up for this."

It took a couple of hours of walking, sticking to the shadows and avoiding the slight early-morning traffic, but we finally saw the warehouses taking shape in front of us.

"We need to stay quiet," Sam whispered, taking the lead. "Someone is probably watching the place."

She was right—something was off as we got nearer to home. We crept from building to building, darting between the open spaces. Voices rang out when we got within earshot, two men were hidden in the shadow cast by our building blocking the morning sun.

"We can't stay out here all day." A cigarette hung from the man's lips as he spoke. The smoke curled around his scruffy face. A second man was leaning in close inspecting the edge of the door for hinges.

"There are no hinges," Cigarette said. "It's solid as a rock."

"Industrial strength," Charlie had called them when he found us the place. "They'll keep anything out." At least he had been telling the truth about that.

"I told you we should shoot it," the second man said, scratching his bald head.

"Well, I left my piece in the car," Cigarette said, gesturing off in the distance towards the far wall.

Baldy was not pleased. "Well, it's not my fault you're an idiot." He shoved Cigarette a little out of the way. "If we come back empty-handed again, the boss is gonna be pissed."

"So, you shoot it then!"

Baldy started to reach behind his back.

Before I knew what was happening, Sam was off like a shot. A blur of pale hair and leather dancing through the open space between the corrugated metal buildings. I took off running right behind her.

Where Sam was silent as a whisper, my size-eleven feet in a pair of old combat boots were not. They made a loud slapping noise on the pavement.

Baldy spun around, scrambling for the revolver tucked under his shirt.

He started to point it in Sam's direction right as she reached him. Before it could fully aim at her, she had her hand on it, twisting it back and up to the sky. Time slowed until I heard the resounding crunch of a finger being broken, then a loud pop when a single shot went off.

Sam shoved Baldy with her free hand while still twisting the gun in her other. It came away into her grasp. She took a quick step back and kicked him in the gut. With a practiced hand, she opened the revolver chamber and emptied the bullets onto the ground. The gun she tossed away, now empty and useless.

As Baldy screamed a war cry, running at Sam, I reached the cigarette guy. I didn't wait; he was still reeling from the gunshot and the indecision of what to do: run to help his friend or stay and fight.

My fist met his jaw and made up his mind for him.

The thing no one told you about a fistfight was that although it hurt like hell getting punched, it hurt almost as much to do the punching. Or at least my hand did.

I shook off the pain and went in for another. Cigarette was expecting it this time and stopped most of my swing with his arm. He threw a left that connected with my ribs, sending me reeling.

Sam and I ended up back-to-back.

Tom had vanished. Typical.

Sam took a ragged breath and spit some blood onto the ground. "You alright?"

"So far," I replied.

We pushed off each other, flinging ourselves back into the fray. I swung at Cigarette's jaw again, but he ducked under it, landing another blow on my ribs. I returned the favor and landed one on his nose with a sharp right. He reeled back, blinking. Blood streamed down his face.

Behind me, there was the sharp crack of a fist, and Sam let out a shout of rage. I had my fight to focus on, but I wouldn't want to be on the receiving end of Sam's frustration.

Cigarette lunged at me. I tried to dodge around him, but he landed a blow right in the gut, knocking the wind out of me. I backed away, gasping for breath.

"Got any ideas?" I called out to Sam.

A shot rang out into the night.

Everyone froze. Cigarette and I backed away from each other. Sam had her hands up in a defensive position, her eyes scanning for the source of the shot. Baldy was on the ground, knocked out cold.

"Hey, dumbass," Tom's voice rang out as he stepped around the corner, holding a pistol. "Why don't you scrape your friend off the ground and get the hell out of here?"

Tom leveled the pistol at Cigarette. Hands as steady as a surgeon. He followed Cigarette with the barrel as the man approached Baldy and picked him up off the ground.

"Oh, and don't bother going for your car." Tom kept aiming at the goons. "The tires don't roll so hot anymore after they had my switchblade in them."

We watched the goons groan and stumble across the warehouse district and away. Tom never stopped pointing the gun at them until they were way out of sight. My head was pounding, my face and ribs throbbing. Sam wasn't as bad off as me, but she was still bleeding from her lip and a cut on her cheek.

"What the hell, Tommy! Where the hell did you get *that?*" I called out to him, motioning to the pistol.

"It was in the Cadillac," Tom said. "Their car was around the corner. I grabbed the one the guy said he left behind." He was trembling some now as the reality of what he'd done started to set in. "I slashed the tires so they couldn't use the car to get back to their friends."

"Also, can someone take this thing?" He held out the gun with two fingers like it was going to bite him. The momentary courage drained out of him.

Sam stepped up and took it from him. Her thumb pushed against the side, and the magazine popped out. She tossed it away into some bushes. With a quick movement, she pulled back the slide, causing a bullet to fly out and clatter across the ground. One last push of a button, and the gun came apart in two pieces. She threw them in separate directions.

I was stunned, mouth agape. "Don't you think we should have kept that?"

"I don't like guns," was all she said.

"Well, they sure seem to. We might not be so lucky next time." I knelt to hunt around for the pieces.

"No, Sticks, no guns. We need to be smarter. One of you will end up shooting the other," Sam said, pulling no punches. "I like you both without bullet holes."

I didn't like it, but even if I found all the pieces, I wouldn't be able to put the thing back together. I had also lost track of where the revolver ended up.

"Shit," I said, my mind coming back to the task we came here for. "We need to check the van. They'll be back with friends, and I'm sure the whole city heard those two gunshots. The cops are probably on the way, too."

I fumbled in my pockets for the keys. I didn't have them. Panic struck me as

Sam stepped forward, jingling them as she did so. She was shaking her head at me, a familiar ritual among all this chaos.

"Anyone know what we're even looking for?" Tom asked.

"I have no idea," I admitted, "but I'm guessing we'll know when we see it."

Chapter 11

Saturday, September 6th, 1986, 9:47 a.m.

I finished locking the door and turned around with a sigh, putting my back against it. I was glad to have a barrier between us and the rest of the world, even if only for a few moments.

The wind had picked up outside, rattling against the garage bay doors, drawing my eyes in that direction. I spotted it across the open ground floor where Sam had parked it—our faithful steed.

"Why the hell is everyone so interested in our hunk of junk?" Tom said, speaking aloud the same thing I was thinking.

"Let's find out," I said.

We started to jog across the open expanse in front of us, the painted cartoon bomb on the side growing more prominent as we approached. The smell of dust hit my nose as we crossed the concrete. Glancing at the floor, Sam's tracks were still visible, walking in the other direction. The last time we were here seemed like ages ago.

When we reached the van, Sam opened the driver's side door and climbed in. She then leaned over and opened the passenger side, then back to open the sliding side door.

"Be quick," she said. "We don't have much time."

The wind rattled the rolling door next to me, startling me into action. Every gust against the metal was a reminder that the clock was ticking. Tony's men or the cops could be here any minute.

We began turning it inside out, pulling off panels, and going through every nook and cranny. I reached under the dash to feel around for anything out of place. We only found an old ham sandwich, green with age, tucked into the back of the glovebox—a science experiment gone wrong.

"There's nothing here!" Tom shouted, kicking the side of the van from the gunner's seat. "What the hell is everyone after?"

"Where else could they hide something?" I reached out to scratch the back of my head, my eyes narrowing. "It would have to be somewhere we wouldn't accidentally find it."

Tom waved dismissively at the vehicle. "I already checked under the hood and under the whole thing."

"What's different?" Sam said with a half-smile on her face. She'd figured it out. "Only one thing is new on this junker."

"The tire!" Tom and I both shouted at the same time.

Sam reached between the seats and grabbed a crowbar. We circled to the back of the van and inspected the tire. It stood out. Its rim was shiny and new, and the treads still had the little stringy bits sticking off them.

Sam wasted no time. She carefully wedged the crowbar between the rim and the tire. The air hissed out all at once when the seal broke. She worked her way around the tire till it hung off the front of the rim.

Tossing the crowbar aside, she pulled on the tire, and it came the rest of the way off with a violent jerk. Sam stepped out of the way as it fell to the floor with a thump. Tom and I backed away as well.

Spilling out onto the floor were bags of white powder—every one of them stamped with a snake eating its tail.

"Son of a bitch, Charlie!" I kicked the tire, cursing his name. His name, and the pain in my toe.

Charlie had given us that spare. It had been the day of our first gig in Winnipeg. He said it was to "Keep his favorite band safe." I was convinced he cared about us. Now, I was questioning everything I knew about him.

"He had us running drugs," I said, my eyes going wide with realization.

Sam climbed into the back, grabbing an ancient duffel bag we had filled with miscellaneous cables and connectors for our gear. She tipped it upside down, dumped the contents all over the back, and tossed it out ahead of her. She picked up the first aid kit, another gift from Charlie, and popped it open. She grabbed rubber gloves from the unused kit and hopped onto the concrete.

"Sticks, hold it open." She gestured to the duffel next to me.

I held the zippered top apart while her gloved hands made quick work of packing up the eight bricks of what had to be cocaine into the duffel.

"Eight kilos," she stated. "That's probably worth over two hundred and fifty thousand dollars."

"Oh my god!" Tom exclaimed. "No wonder they were shooting at us. What the hell are we going to do?"

"We need to pack it up and disappear." She zipped the bag closed and slung it over her shoulder. "What's next?"

"We need to hide it," I said. "I have an idea."

I led the way, checking around the door for anyone who might be lurking there. No one was around, so I darted out and made my way between the warehouses. Several were abandoned like ours. We made our way to the far end of a decrepit old building with the rusted sheet metal walls peeling back from the frame. I held the corner up to let Tom and Sam climb in.

"I've never seen anyone parked by this one," I said. "I think it's unused."

My eyes combed through the contents of the building. Old crates and dust. That was about it. Through the center of the building was a drainage ditch covered by heavy iron grates. I made my way over to them and strained to lift one of the plates out. Sam stepped in and assisted me after handing Tom the duffel bag. He held it out like it was going to bite him.

The grate let out a scream of protest as it came free. I nodded at Tom, and he placed the bag in the uncovered ditch.

"That should do it," I said, putting the grate back in place. "For now anyway."

The windows suddenly darkened, dimming the space around us. We ducked instinctively. I crab-walked over to peek out, trying to stay unseen. Through years of caked on gunk, I saw a pair of black Cadillacs pull past, headed for our place.

"They're back with reinforcements."

"Perfect." Tom sighed. "What do we do now?"

"We make ourselves scarce before they find us."

I moved away from the window facing our section of the warehouses and surveyed our handiwork one last time. The duffel bag was hidden out of sight, and there were no visible tracks we'd left behind. It would have to do.

The door on the opposite wall sat slightly ajar. The wind whistled through the crack, howling like a mad dog snapping at our heels.

"You ready?" I asked as if we had a choice.

"Ready," Sam said, and Tom muttered the same word.

I pulled the door slightly more open, enough to squeeze through, making a wish that it wouldn't squeak and alert everyone to our presence. That was at least one granted.

We made our way out into the windy driveways between warehouses. None of Tony's men were in sight. They must still be trying to find us at our place.

"We need to hurry," Sam whispered. "They're going to be looking for us soon. We need to be gone."

I nodded and took the lead. The warehouse district's grime clung to the air, filling my lungs as I ushered Tom and Sam through the maze of alleys. Shadows stretched out like twisted fingers, clawing at us.

I tried to shake the fear running up my spine as we made our way to the end of all the buildings. Sam's head swiveled like an owl looking for prey, eyes taking in every angle around us. No signs of anyone yet. We made it to the side street and paused to catch our breath.

"Where the hell are we going?" Tom asked. "We've got no one left to help us."

"We gotta stay out of sight, somewhere off the radar," I said, trying to take charge. "There's gotta be some way out of this mess."

Briefly illuminated by the morning sun we raced across the street. Once on the other side, we all huddled in the shadows again, listening. Minutes passed with my nerves on edge, feeling every second drag on.

"I don't think anyone spotted us." Sam turned her attention to me. "Where to?"

I racked my brains, trying to come up with where to go. Looking at my two bandmates, Tom was panting, eyes roving over the other side of the street. Sam was stoic and relaxed, deferring to me for what came next. Only one place came to mind.

"Back to the beginning, I guess." I cracked a smile despite myself.

"Oh, no... not that place," Tom said as if his worst nightmare was coming true.

"Anywhere is better than here," I answered.

The neon sign of the seedy motel flickered in the afternoon sun. It couldn't decide if there was vacancy or not. By the look of the parking lot, I'd say our chances were good.

A couple of tired-looking prostitutes didn't even bother to approach us as we walked up.

"Sticks, man... Why this place?" Tom groaned. "Do you remember the size of the rat we saw here? It was like a small cat."

"It's not the nicest place, but we haven't been back since we all met." I put my hand on Tom's shoulder. "No one would link us to this place. Plus, we walked all day to get here. I'm not going anywhere else."

"Fine. One night, then we need to find somewhere else to sleep. My skin is already crawling."

"Let's get inside," Sam said, her voice almost inaudible over the barking dogs and the thumping music from one of the distant rooms.

"Remember, we're regular folks looking for a place to crash," I said, attempting to convince myself as much as them. We couldn't afford to draw any attention, not with the cops and Big Tony both gunning for us.

Regular folks was a bit of a stretch for us, but we tried to act casual as we stepped into the dingy lobby. The clerk eyed us up and down, his gaze lingering on Tom's blue hair before looking Sam up and down in a manner I was guessing she didn't appreciate.

He didn't remember us. We'd been here once before but didn't spend the night. He hadn't changed a bit. He was still a cross between the crypt keeper and Riff Raff from *The Rocky Horror Picture Show*.

"Need some rooms?" he croaked out.

"One room. Two beds and a cot," I answered.

His eyes passed over all three of us again, and he shrugged and sniffed like he had a cold. "Whatever you're into, it's none of my business. Don't wreck my room."

He handed over a key attached to an oversized plastic keychain that displayed our room number on it. "Number twelve. No bullshit, no drugs, no parties. Keep it down." He sniffed again, rubbing his nose while he spat the well-rehearsed schtick at us and pointed at the door.

"A pleasure as always," Tom said and bowed before he turned to leave.

We made our way down to the room and let ourselves in. The scent of cheap motel assaulted our senses. Stale, sweaty, and desperate.

"I'll take the cot," Tom said, wheeling the rusty old thing out of the corner where it was stashed. "It's probably the only thing without a stain." It screeched a rusty complaint when he unfolded it.

"Such a gentleman." Sam chuckled at Tom.

He went a little pink around the ears. "Sorry, Sam. You can have it if you want."

"I'm messing with you. I wouldn't fit anyway. I'd rather not have my feet hanging over the floor." She quirked a smile. "Who knows what would nibble on my toes in this place?"

"Oh, man, you had to say that? Really?" Tom slumped down sitting on the cot, looking especially dejected. His eyes found mine after a moment. "Sticks, what are we doing, man? We can't run forever."

I breathed deep, trying to settle the fear that was roiling inside my belly. "We can do this," I insisted. "We've got each other's backs, and that's what matters."

"That's not going to stop a bullet."

"Listen, I get it. But we've got leverage. Big Tony's guys have seen the van; they know we have the drugs. He won't kill us until he gets his stash back." I hoped that was true.

"What about Harris?" Sam said.

"Yeah, I haven't forgotten about him," I replied, hanging my head in frustration. My mind was blank, as lost and confused as they felt. There was no way I was going to let them know that, though. I didn't want to let them down. Guilt pulsed through me. My thoughts strayed back to a few days ago. *I'm going to leave the band. I'm going to let them down.*

I shook the thought out of my head. There was no time for that. We needed a plan, a way out of this.

"I'm not sure yet." I said, "I need some sleep. My...everything is running on empty."

"You and me both," Tom said, falling back onto the cot.

We settled in. I pulled back the covers on my bed and much to my surprise, it was almost stain-free. Sam didn't even care. She climbed in to hers without looking. As my head settled on the pillow, I started to doze. Tom's voice pulled me out of it.

"Sticks, you remember the last time we were here?"

"Yeah, don't worry about it, man. I'm sure that rat is dead by now."

"No, not that. That was the day it all started. That was our first day as Bombs Away."

"Yeah, I remember. That was a good day," I said, words slurring with drowsiness.

"It was a good day," Tom agreed, yawning.

I drifted off to sleep with memories of the past running through my head.

Chapter 12

Friday, July 27th, 1984, 2:16 p.m.

"This day sucks," Tom growled, his mohawk casting a shadow over the peeling wallpaper as he slumped back on the rickety motel bed. "Did you see the size of that damn rat?"

"You need to let it go, man. He was as scared of you as you were of him." I had to admit, though, that rat was huge.

We'd been able to scrape together enough crumpled bills to rent a room at this lovely establishment. The front desk clerk, all leathery, with his rising-from-beyond-the-grave good looks, had leered at us when we asked to rent the room by the hour. His snide comment as we'd made our way out the door to our room rang in our ears for the rest of the day.

We didn't have a rehearsal space yet, but we needed a place to hold auditions, and we needed a bass player.

"This place reeks of cigarettes and broken dreams," I muttered, tapping out a rhythm on my thigh with restless fingers. The room was a time capsule of tacky decor. *We'll call it "Brady Bunch Chic," but Alice would have been pissed to see it in this state.*

"No one is going to come," Tom said, eyeing the door like it owed him money. "This whole audition thing is a bust."

"Well, you convinced me to come," I told him, though I wasn't enthusiastic about our prospects either. "Someone's going to want to jam with us. They'll show up."

But as minutes ticked by into an eternity, the silence grew, gnawing at the edges of our confidence.

I should have never left jazz for this, I caught myself thinking, then shoved the thought away. I didn't mean that. Jazz had been my life; it was creativity and syncing up with other musicians, and it was a big part of who I was for a while. It didn't make me happy, though. When I met Tom and got introduced to the punk scene, my eyes were opened. It was raw power turned into sound. There was no way I was turning back now.

A soft knock broke the tension.

"Finally!" Tom said, sitting up with renewed interest. He nodded to the door, and I followed his gaze as he said, "Showtime."

The door creaked open, and the sliver of sunlight that came in tried its best to brighten all the shabby corners of the room. Even the sun could only do so much.

My eyes adjusted to the change in light. Silhouetted in front of us was what could only be described as the love child of Sid Vicious and a deranged peacock. Our first auditionee strode into the room with more swagger than a drunk on a tightrope. I thought that was a good song title, jotting down "Tightrope" in the notepad next to me. I turned my attention from the notebook as he introduced himself.

"Name's Jimmy. Jimmy Rotten." He flashed a grin that had seen more bar fights than dentists. His voice rang with an accent like *Mary Poppins'* chimney sweep. It wanted to sound English, but a midwestern twang still made it through.

"Original," Tom deadpanned. I stifled a snort.

"Got any experience?" I asked, raising an eyebrow.

"Experience? Mate, I live and breathe punk. I've been kicked out of every dive in this city," Jimmy boasted, his accent beginning to fall apart the more he said. He fumbled with the latches on his guitar case until it sprung open.

"Let's see what you've got." Tom sighed, crossing his arms and waiting for Jimmy to play.

He strapped on his guitar, a Fender P-Bass that had almost certainly never been touched. He started to pluck out a few notes. It sounded like it had never been tuned, either. He reached up and tweaked one of the pegs, only a fraction. He plucked another note no better than the last and nodded like it was perfect.

If what came next was considered music of any kind, I was in the wrong business. It was a thumping, out-of-tune, disjointed mess.

"Hey, watch it!" I barked, the lamp in the corner getting knocked over as he flailed around, pretending he was on stage.

"Sorry, man," he said, not sounding sorry at all. "That's the power of the music flowing through me."

"I think that's enough," Tom said, rolling his eyes and leaning forward from the edge of the bed, exasperated.

"Yeah, we've had enough," I said. "We'll let you know."

"Your loss," Jimmy huffed, putting his instrument away and storming out with far too much misplaced confidence.

"Let's hope the next one knows what a fretboard is." Tom flopped back on the grimy mattress.

A few minutes later, the door blasted open like the SWAT team was making a bust. A shaved head and a leather jacket loomed in the door frame.

"Name's Dee," the man announced as if we were supposed to know him. He ran his hands over his scalp, an unconscious movement from a past with much more hair.

"Dee, show us what you got," Tom said, his voice flat, a stark contrast to the bold entrance. Our hopefulness before the first audition was gone, replaced by a wariness that hovered around, mixing with the stench of stale cigarettes.

Dee plugged in, cranked the amp, and, without asking, started moving the EQ settings all over the place. He pranced around as he played, oblivious to the grimaces he was putting on our faces. Each slap of the strings caused the grimaces to deepen.

"Ever been in a band before?" I asked once there was a break in the noise, lest he mistake our silence for awe.

"Tons," he shot back, flashing a grin that sparkled with unearned confidence. "I'm the best you're gonna find in this dump of a city."

"Is that so?" Tom arched an eyebrow. He stood up, and shrugged his shoulders, a smirk playing on his lips. "From where I'm sitting, it sounds like you couldn't find the rhythm if it was stapled to your jacket."

Tom, a chicken about most things, did not pull punches when it came to his music. He didn't want just anyone in this band. They had to check all the boxes.

"Whatever," Dee muttered, unplugging his bass with a dramatic flourish that made the amp teeter and almost come crashing down. "When I'm famous, you'll wish you had me."

"Sure," I said as the door slammed behind him, the pictures on the walls tipped further askew. "Famous for clearing out clubs."

"Sticks, man, if this next one is a dud..." Tom let the sentence hang, but I knew what he meant. We'd be a two-person act if we didn't find a bassist soon. It was doable, but we were looking for a different sound. If we couldn't fill this spot, this band would break up before it even started.

"Let's hope the third time's the charm," I said, staring at the door with defiance and desperation. "Can't get much worse, can it?"

"*Never* say that!" Tom scolded. "It's like begging the universe to kick you in the teeth."

I shifted from the disgusting bed to the moldy couch. Dust rose in clouds around me when I sat. My fingers started drumming out patterns on the battered armrest, foam sticking through the frayed material threatening to burst at any moment.

Tom paced back and forth in the tiny room, his mohawk slicing through the air like a shark's fin. I began to think this third guy was going to flake on us.

"What's the last one's name?" I asked, trying to pass some time.

"Derick, I think." Tom was distracted. He was lost in his thoughts, probably imagining the worst like I was.

"I'm going to open the door." I said, the hinges creaked and protested like bad sound effects from a horror movie. I wedged a doorstop under it. "It'll be more inviting that way." At that point, I was willing to teach a total stranger how to play.

Before I got back to the couch, someone approached the door, almost at a run from the sound of it. Tom and I both held our breath in anticipation.

This better be Derick.

But a woman walked in. Not Derick, then. She almost had to duck to come through the door. She peered behind her like someone was chasing her. Her blond hair covered half her face; the other half of her head was shaved. She closed the door behind her, locked it, and spun to face us. One pale blue eye studied us, studied the room.

"Who's chasing you, the ghost of auditions past?" I asked, unable to shake off the odd sense of urgency that clung to her.

"She's the talent police," Tom joked, "looking for those other two idiots who were here earlier. I'm guessing you're not Derrick, though?"

"Sorry, not Derrick," she said, looking like she was about to bolt the first chance she got. Tall, over six feet for sure. She wore a leather jacket hanging casually open over a torn t-shirt that fit her like a glove. She had all the trappings of a supermodel, but I sensed something else beyond her appearance. She had a kind of energy that I couldn't put a finger on.

I shook off the idea; it was a long day making me imagine things. After a moment, she seemed like she'd made a decision and said, "Am I late?" Her voice had an accent. It was foreign, but I couldn't place it.

"Late? Honey, if you can play, I don't care what time you get here," Tom said, trying to act suave.

"Call me *honey* one more time, and you won't be able to hold that guitar you've got."

That was it, the thing I was sensing—danger. She seemed dangerous. She was like a cat, ready to swat at anything that set her off. Not a house cat, though. I was talking big cats. The ones you saw at the zoo or heard David Attenborough talking about.

Tom raised his hands. "Sorry, it's been a long day. Won't happen again." He gestured to our spare bass we brought in case the auditionees came without one. It was nothing special; we'd just picked up a well-used Ibanez at a pawn shop for the occasion.

She eyed it up and down and picked it up, holding it out to examine it like it was a foreign object to her. "Is it like an upright?" she asked, turning the bass around in her hands to get a better look at it.

"Sort of..." I was confused. Was she a musician?

She plucked a couple of the strings. Then, all four.

"Same tuning." She held down strings on a couple of frets, struck more notes, and froze. It was like her ears perked up. Her head spun to look at the window.

"You okay?" I asked.

"Shhh!" she hissed.

I stopped, listening. I didn't hear anything.

Then a moment later, footsteps.

Tom and I glanced at each other. Derick? They passed our room, and our auditionee took a breath.

"Are you in some kind of trouble?" Tom asked. "Do you need us to call someone for you?"

Her head snapped toward us, and she held a finger to her lips. She got up from the chair and moved over to the door, not making a sound. She held the bass at her side like a weapon, standing at the ready.

The footsteps grew louder until they stopped at the room next to us. Then more movement, and they stopped outside our door. The knob rattled a little. Our auditionee tensed and held the guitar at the ready.

Whoever it was moved on, and it was like all the tension drained from the room.

"What the hell was that?" Tom's voice broke the silence. "Are you okay?"

"Thought I saw someone out there I'd rather avoid," she said, peeking out of the curtain next to the door. "But it's just the leathery man from the front desk."

"We don't want any trouble," I said, echoing what I knew Tom was thinking.

"No trouble," she said. "I don't like trouble either."

She made her way back over to one of the chairs. Sat down and propped the bass on one of her knees, plugging it into the amp. She tested a few more frets, her eyes closed. She reached up and turned a tuning knob while plucking the string. Unlike our friend Jimmy, she knew what she was doing. She plucked all four strings. All in tune. She gave a satisfied "hmmm".

She then launched into a complicated run of several scales, all the way up and down the fretboard. Stopping for a moment, she closed her eyes, took a deep breath, and then really got started.

Tom and I both locked eyes, our mouths saying, "Holy shit" at the same time.

I remembered thinking that it was what being hustled must be like. She came in here acting like she'd never seen a guitar before, but then she played like she was born to it. She slowed down and came to a stop. She was smiling behind the wall of hair, with one turned-up corner of her lips visible.

"Who are you?" Tom asked, still in shock.

She shrugged. "I'm just Sam,"

"Well, Sam." I walked up to her with my hand extended. "Do you like punk?"

Her smile grew bigger as we shook hands.

"Welcome to Bombs Away, *just* Sam."

Chapter 13

Sunday, September 7th, 1986, 6:26 a.m.

I woke up with the memories swimming all around me. This hotel was where it all started. Sam and Tom were still sleeping, but I knew they would be awake soon from their restless movements.

I rose to my feet and walked over to the window. I peeked between the threadbare curtains, the same design as the last time we were here, and surveyed the parking lot. Nothing was out of place.

Making my way to the tiny dusty chair in one corner of the room, I sat in silence, trying not to wake the others. My head reeled with the past few days' events, and a familiar feeling returned to the pit of my stomach.

What was I doing? We'd been "surviving" for the last couple of years. Trying to make ends meet gigging between here and Canada. Did we even earn any of that, or was it handed to us so we would sneak drugs across the border without knowing it?

I didn't think I could do it anymore. If we made it out of this alive, I was done. Charlie had done this to us. Made us criminals, made fools of us.

Charlie. The image of his body lying on the floor with one of my drumsticks in his eye flashed through my head. My elbows rested on my knees, my head in my hands. I let out a sigh, trying to process everything.

"Sticks, you alright?" Sam said groggily, sitting up in her bed.

"Yeah, it's all getting to me," lifting my head to stare at nothing. "Charlie used us."

"It's possible." She swung her legs out from under the covers to sit on the side of the bed facing my chair. "They might have forced him to do it."

"Still doesn't sit right," I said, rubbing my fingers across the threadbare upholstery. "I mean, we've been through some shit, but this? It's too much."

"You said it yourself; we need to keep going. We're too close."

She was right, but I didn't want to be reasonable right now. "Is it worth it, though?" I saw Tom sitting up as I said it, our conversation waking him.

"Is what worth it?" he asked.

"All of it." I shrugged.

"We've got to keep going," Tom said, slapping his hands on the cot, stirring up a cloud of dust that choked him up. He coughed out, "for the band."

I snorted and hung my head, then turned away from him as I looked back up—anything to avoid his eyes. I didn't want to see his face.

"Is this band even real?" I wondered aloud. "Or did Charlie push us along to be his mules?"

The silence in the room lingered far longer than I would have liked. I wanted Tom to rage and scream at me.

"You're an idiot," Sam said, shaking her head.

"*And* you're an asshole," Tom spoke evenly. He didn't raise his voice. That was the worst part. I still couldn't make eye contact with him. He got up from the bed and stomped over to me. "Of course, the band is real. We worked our asses off. You don't get to call our band fake."

"I'm sorry, you're right. I just... I can't help but think about how Charlie used us," I said, staring up at the ceiling. The moldy water-stained tiles looked like a really depressing Rorschach ink blot test.

"Charlie using us has nothing to do with the band," Sam retorted, her voice like daggers. "We need to solve this."

"Or die trying?" I asked.

Sam shrugged. "Or we solve the damn thing, and we keep playing."

"I'm not sure I can." I wanted to say it but couldn't make the words come out.

"Not sure you can what?" Tom, his voice now ratcheting up in volume with each word.

I had to do this. It had been rattling around in my head for days. "I'm not sure I can keep doing it, the music thing."

"You're unbelievable." The air around Tom crackled with tension. "We've had our struggles, but we're doing it. We're playing shows. People show up. We're together!" His complexion grew redder while his arms flailed around. "So we're not rocking out in stadiums. Who cares? We've got a roof over our heads; we're doing something most people only dream about. Would you rather go back to waiting tables and drumming one night a week in a jazz club?"

"I'm tired," I admitted. "Charlie betrayed us. This whole thing is doing its best to get pinned on me."

"They're trying to pin it on all of us," Sam said. "Not you."

"It was my drumstick!" I burst out. "You two could walk away. In fact, you probably should."

Sam was up on her feet, pure fury on her face. "We could leave, Sticks, but we're not going to. We're a team. We're in this together—till the end. You don't get to leave like this means nothing."

Sam's voice cracked like a whip around me. I'd never seen her angry like this. I backed away from her wrath and held my hands in front of me, trying to put a barrier between myself and the storm I had stirred up.

"I'm... I'm trying to decide what's best for me," I said, taking another small step backward.

"What's best for *you*?" Tom shouted. "You're not hearing us. It's not you or me. It's *we—us*. We're family, you moron."

Sam's face softened as well. Her voice lowered. "You should have told us right away when you started thinking about this."

"I wanted to." My voice trembled. "I was going to talk to you about it after Winnipeg. We called Charlie and he told us about The Palms, and I forgot all about it for a while."

"Yeah, because then the shit hit the fan," Tom said. At least he wasn't yelling.

"Listen, I... I'm sorry. I'm being an idiot. This is all getting to me."

Tom glared at me. "You're right. You are being an idiot."

"Agreed," Sam said.

"How about that? We all agree on something." Tom smiled. "You're an idiot. It's a consensus."

I couldn't help but crack a smile, too. "I am sorry. When we're out of all this, let's come up with a plan for us moving forward. We need to stop with the dive clubs and shows to twenty people in another country."

"That's what we want too." Sam pulled us both into a hug. "No more idiots."

"That's a good song title," I said, hugging them back.

The three of us lingered in the hug for a moment, then pulled away. We stood in the center of the crappy hotel room awkwardly.

"We need to come up with something, though. I've been winging it, and we're getting nowhere."

"Come on, this place is five stars," Tom joked.

"I meant stuck between Big Tony and the cops," I said.

Sam's head snapped up. "Then we should move out of the way."

"What do you mean?" Tom asked.

Sam paced the room as she spoke. "Big Tony was using Charlie and us to smuggle his drugs into the country, right?"

"Right," Tom and I answered simultaneously.

"And it somehow got him killed."

"Yeah..." We were trying to follow her train of thought, but I needed to figure out what station she was headed for.

"Detective Harris wants the killer." She sped up trying to wear a line into the carpet of the tiny room. I noticed the more she said, the more pronounced her accent became. "We have Big Tony's drugs."

"Yeah, which I still think is a horrible idea," Tom said, but it didn't break Sam's flow.

"So, let's use that to our advantage. We fill in the detective. We use the drugs to draw out Tony, and Harris gets his man."

"You think he's going to buy that?" I asked.

"It's the truth," she said. "Mostly... well, as much truth as we have right now."

As Sam's pacing slowed, she almost seemed shocked at how much she'd been speaking. She sat back on the edge of the bed and waited for us to digest what she'd said.

"It's more of a plan than we have right now," I said, my jaw hurting from clenching my teeth together in anxiety, "but I'm not sure how we'll convince Harris to go along with it. He and the boys in blue already think we're guilty."

"If we give him the bigger fish, that'll help," Tom said. "We didn't do it. He won't believe that right away, but he'll stop and think about it when we lay out our story, and he realizes he can take down Big Tony."

"I like it a lot, but we're forgetting one thing. We're all assuming that Harris isn't dirty and is not already in Big Tony's pocket."

"Shit." Tom shook his head. "I hadn't thought of that. So, if we do one thing, Big Tony kills us; if we do the other, the cops will."

"Harris isn't dirty," Sam said with complete conviction—no trace of doubt in her voice.

"How can you know that?" I asked. "We only talked to him once. How can you be sure he's not in Tony's pocket?"

"I know it. I can tell," she insisted.

"You know, we've never asked, and I'm not going to now, but someday, I'd love to figure out how know the things you know."

She gave a nonchalant shrug. "Someday."

"Sam's mysterious past will have to wait." Tom's brow furrowed, and he exhaled sharply. "What do we do right now?"

"It's early," I said. "We wait."

"Like a duck. A duck that's sitting." Tom threw his hands in the air. Done with the conversation, he flopped down on the bed. After a moment, he sat back up. "Also, you're not leaving the band. When this is over, we're getting back on track, and we'll be bigger than ever."

Sam busied herself going through her pockets and what few belongings she had with her. Tom stared at the ceiling, playing air guitar. I was glad I had them and that even Tom seemed to think we would make it through this.

Did Charlie like our band at all? Was he even a manager, or was it all a cover to find someone to smuggle coke? Doubts filled me, and I couldn't get them out of my head.

My mind strayed to flashes of Charlie's body, then to memories of us all laughing together. Of getting the news of our next gig from him. That time, he'd had a few "Bombs Away" T-shirts done up, and we'd felt like we'd "made it" by having merch to sell.

The room's stagnant air lingered in my nose like an unwelcome guest. The couch and chair were threadbare, and the bed linens were dirty. Charlie would have never put us up in a place like this.

The more I thought about it, the more I convinced myself Charlie cared. Big Tony must have had something on him, forcing him to do it. I wasn't sure why, but that made me feel a lot better.

I focused on that, and the fear and guilt fell away, hiding for now in some dark corner of my mind. It was time to finish this, to solve it for Charlie. I settled into my chair. I had my friends, and we hadn't been busted yet. We could do this. As long as we stuck together, we'd make it through.

Chapter 14

Sunday, September 7th, 1986, 10:26 a.m.

The morning sun crept through the dusty curtains, casting a pale light on the worn carpet as I walked back in from the bathroom. I wiped my hands down the front of my shirt. There was no way I was touching the towels in this place. The room darkened for a moment when a shadow passed by the window, blocking the light for a second.

"Sticks," Tom called out from across the room. He halted his scribbling on the notepad he'd gotten from the bedside table, and narrowed his eyes. "Did you notice that creepy front desk guy keeps passing by our room?"

"Really?" I leaned out from the chair to try and find a better angle. Sure enough, he was passing by again. "He's got a thing for Sam," I joked, trying to brush off the unease tickling the edges of my mind. "That or he's doing his job."

Several car tires screeched to a halt outside in the parking lot. Jolting up from my chair, I hurried over to the window.

Three black Cadillacs had pulled up right outside our door.

"Fuck!" I cursed, my thoughts running wild. They found us. Big Tony's henchmen, dressed in black sport coats with tattoos of a serpent eating its tail peeking up above their collars. They spread out, positioning themselves around the entrance to our room.

"Skeevy front desk guy sold us out. Does Tony own everyone in this town?" Tom's voice was shaking with anger, which was better than fear, in any case.

"We need to go now. Go, go!" My voice cracked with stress. As I turned to the others, I saw the fear in their eyes and knew they understood.

We started to edge away from the window when there were several clicks from outside, one after the other.

"*DOWN!*" Sam barked out as she tackled both Tom and me to the ground.

The world exploded around us. Glass and bits of drywall rained down as a hail of bullets tore through the room.

"Keep your heads down," Sam called out when the bullets stopped.

Light spilled in through the torn curtains and a hundred new holes in the walls and front door.

The weight of our predicament closed in on us like a vise. I guess Tony didn't care if he got his drugs first, he just wanted us dead. The room seemed to shrink around me, the acrid scent of gunpowder filling my nostrils. We had to move—and fast.

"Out the back!" I suggested, my mind racing for an escape route. "Through the bathroom window."

"Let's go!" Tom agreed, his voice shaking but resolute.

Sam nodded, and we crawled across the floor like a trio of punk rock commandos, dodging shards of glass and bullets along the way.

"He sold us out," Sam muttered, her voice venomous. "When we're out of this, I'm gonna tear his throat out."

"I'll help," Tom added, his face pale. "But first, let's focus on staying alive."

We pushed into the tiny cubicle of a bathroom—nothing more than a stand-up shower, a sink, and a toilet. We did our best to squeeze in around the fixtures. It was as clean as you'd expect in a place like this. The window in question was tiny.

Sam ran up to it and inspected it. It was more like half a window, with ancient peeling paint and a tiny crank on the bottom. She started to work the crank in circles, and the window squeaked open, a few centimeters every rotation.

"We don't have time for this," I muttered imagining those goons busting through the door any moment.

"Give me a second!" Sam said, concentrating on what she was doing. The window opened in slow motion. Once it had moved enough that she had a place to grip it on the top and bottom, she took in a deep breath and, in a single pull, ripped the window right out of its frame. She tossed it aside into the shower and gestured to the opening. "Ladies first."

As Tom climbed through, he gaped at Sam like he'd seen a ghost. "How did you…?"

"Termites and old wood," she answered, shrugging. "Let's move."

Tom squeezed through. Then, I hopped out one leg at a time, scraping my back and front along the splintered edges. Sam lithely stepped through, contorting her body to make it look easy. We had made it into the alley behind the motel. The smell of trash and piss filled our nostrils. *I'm so glad we came back to this place. It was lovely inside and out.*

From where we crouched below the window, a thunderous crash reached our ears. There went the door. The crypt keeper would not be thrilled. I motioned to the others, and we sprinted down the back side of the motel and away from the guns. We could escape those for the moment. The danger, though, was the one thing that we weren't able to outrun.

There was frantic yelling from back in the direction of our room. I didn't risk a glance, but I could hear a voice say, "I'm stuck. Someone pull me the hell out of this."

I guess living on punk rock and ramen had made us leaner than the cocaine-and-crime diet.

Our boots hit the cold, wet pavement with a repetitive smacking sound. I winced at the noise. It was like a starter pistol going off in our race for survival.

"Cut through the back alleys," Sam called out in a harsh whisper. She split to her right down a narrow space between two brick buildings.

"We're running out of alleys," I told Sam. "We're almost out of the city. The buildings are a little thin here."

We ducked down behind a dumpster to catch our breath.

"All this running is bullshit," Tom gasped out between breaths. "I didn't sign up for this."

"None of us did," Sam replied, her eyes scanning the street ahead for any signs of danger. "We need to figure out our next steps."

"Everywhere we go, they track us down," I said, breathing heavily, the stench of trash and rot filling my nostrils. "In a year, this guy owns the city. How is that possible?"

Tom answered my rhetorical question. "Something about money and the root of all evil."

I went through our options in my head. Our place was out. Mick had burned us already. A hotel we hadn't been to in a couple of years hadn't worked either. I recalled the front desk guy sniffing. Not a cold then, a coke habit.

"Our only option is to disappear," I said, rubbing the back of my neck, "at least for a little while. We can head to Madison, hide out, and try to figure this all out."

"How the hell are we getting out of town?" Tom asked. "Our van is torn apart and surrounded by goons. Mick's car is god knows where by now."

"We're going to have to come up with something. Steal it, whatever." I was out of ideas.

"So, to get away from criminals, we need to become criminals? We already stole one car, let's not push our luck."

"I'm all ears, Tom." I raised my palms to him in a "the floor is yours" gesture.

He sat thinking for a moment, cracking his knuckles to release some tension. He opened his mouth to speak, but before he did, blasts of police sirens sounded. He stopped, stunned to silence.

Our eyes darted around, waiting for the police to come bearing down on us. The sirens moved down the street, headed to the motel.

"We need to move," I said. "We can't stay behind this dumpster forever."

I stood up and prepared to step out from our hiding place. Sam, pulling my arm, tugged me back down. She held a finger to her lips.

The sirens faded, then stopped as they pulled into the hotel. Cars passed on the street. A dog barked in the distance, then footsteps. It sounded like two or three people.

"Spread out. They didn't get too far," a thick Chicago accent said.

I held my breath, shrinking against the brick wall behind the dumpster. I saw Tom doing the same thing. Sam was like a coiled spring. She was ready to explode into action if she needed to. For now, though, she sat still, not moving a muscle. The only thing making any motion at all was her eyes.

"You think the others got out before the pigs showed up?" another voice asked the first.

"Not our problem."

They were close, but I couldn't see anything from where I was. I imagined they were right on the other side of the dumpster. "Keep looking. If we don't find these three, the boss is gonna be pissed."

Their conversation got louder, echoing off the walls around us. They stalked past us, oblivious to our presence.

"What makes these three so important?" Number Two said.

"You got a death wish or something?" Number One didn't sound pleased. "What's with all the questions? The boss says, 'Find 'em,' so we find 'em."

"I'm only wonderin', that's all," Number Two answered. "Seems like a lot to go through for a couple of punks."

They had reached the end of the alley. I poked my head out and saw their backs. They were just standing there, looking back and forth on the street. I pulled my head back in before they turned around.

"For real, though." Number Two was still talking as they walked back toward us again. "What are we doing here that we couldn't do in Chicago? I haven't had a decent piece of pizza since we got here."

"You need to shut the hell up," Number One said as they walked in front of the dumpster again. The distraction the talker was causing was the only reason they didn't notice us. They finally reached the other end and turned left, away from the hotel.

Once I was sure they were out of earshot, I whispered, "Well, we can't go that way now."

"So, it's out in the open on the street or back to the hotel," Sam said.

"Great," Tom muttered. "So it's spotted by everyone walking in broad daylight or right to jail if we go to the hotel. I'm not feeling enthusiastic about these odds."

"I say we go to the main street," I suggested, making the decision no one else wanted to.

"The street, then what?" Tom questioned.

"I think we need to turn ourselves in." I said, "We can't run forever. Sam's plan could work. We need to explain and hope that Harris will see reason. "

"How are we going to do that and not get shot?" Tom replied.

"I don't know, but I'm sick of running," I said. "We're innocent. I don't trust them, but at least the cops haven't shot at us."

"Yet," Tom pointed out. "They still might if they have the chance."

"I agree, they might. I don't think Harris would, though." I hoped Sam was right about him.

"This is a bad idea." Tom crossed his arms tightly, his jaw clenched in apprehension. "We can't be sure if he's on our side, and even if he is, how can we know he'll be the one to find us?"

"If we run, they'll find us at some point, no matter what," I said. "And I'm tired."

"So," Tom said, "what next?"

"Let's find a payphone and call Harris." I stood up, scanning in every direction. I half expected one of the goons to jump out and start firing at us.

Tom and Sam reluctantly followed me. I saw a payphone about a block down on the corner. Hand in pockets, head down, I led the way. Tom had his collar pulled up to hide his face. However, it did nothing to hide his towering blue hair. Next Christmas, I vowed to buy him a hat.

We reached the end of the street, and I picked up the receiver. I reached out to call the operator, and before my hand ever touched the phone, there was a metallic *click* behind me.

Sam spun around, hands up in front of her, about to take a swing.

I turned my head to see Harris with a revolver pointed at us.

"Bombs Away. Fancy meeting you here. You're all under arrest for the murder of Charles Fitzpatrick."

Chapter 15

Sunday, September 7th, 1986, 10:40 a.m.

The metal cuffs bit into my wrists as Detective Harris's vice grip closed them with a *click* that echoed in my eardrums. "You have the right to remain silent," he barked, his voice sharp as the glare from his badge.

Tom, Sam, and I exchanged looks, a cocktail of shock and panic as they were cuffed.

"Anything you say can and will be used against you in a court of law..." Harris said, but his words blurred into the background noise around me.

We shuffled forward, our hands clasped by the cuffs in front of us. A little way down the road, a black and white was parked. As we approached it, I noticed a black Cadillac further down the street. Two goons leaned against it, watching everything. When they saw me looking, they both smirked and waved while we were loaded into the cruiser's back seat. Cold dread ran through my veins.

They didn't seem worried they were losing us. They knew right where we were now.

"Watch your head," Harris grunted, though his shove suggested he'd enjoy it if I didn't.

I ducked into the car, the scent of stale coffee and sweat greeting me like an old roadie. Tom slid in next to me, shoved by another officer. Sam lowered herself into the car on the other side of me after shaking off Harris's hand and glaring at him.

My head was bowed, not out of shame but disbelief. I let out a snort at the ridiculousness of it all. We were about to call and turn ourselves in, and they grabbed us. Now they had us packed like sardines in the back of a cruiser, handcuffed and under arrest for a murder we didn't commit.

"Enjoying the view?" Harris sneered, catching my eye in the mirror. His piercing grey-eyed gaze could've frozen hell over, but I didn't want to give him the satisfaction of seeing me sweat.

"You've bought me jewelry," I said, showing him the cuffs. "Now we're going for a drive? If I didn't know better, I'd think you fancied me."

The detective's lips twitched into a frown, his jaw setting in a way that told me he was suspicious of my act. It didn't matter what I said. He'd already made up his mind about us, and he could see right through my bullshit.

The car's vinyl seat clung to my skin anywhere it touched. I was wedged in between Tom and Sam, the metal of the cuffs cutting off the circulation to my hands. My fingers were curled into tight fists, my knuckles white with tension. The accusation still rattled around in my head. *Murder.* When Harris said it out loud, it somehow made this more real.

"Man, this is bullshit," I muttered, glaring at the cage separating us from the front of the car. "We didn't do jack."

Tom, rubbing his palms against his pant legs, his face flickering with that familiar fear, swallowed hard. "Sticks," he whispered, his voice barely carrying over the engine's hum. "This is messed up, real messed up."

"Tell me about it," I replied, though I could tell he was thinking about more than the handcuffs and the cold stares from Harris in the front seat. I saw his eyes move to the side of the street where the goons had been outside their car, observing us.

Sam, pressed against my side, shot us a glare that could've cut glass. It was her way of saying, "Keep it together." She didn't need words; her icy blue gaze would have been enough to stop us in our tracks. She decided to use them anyway. "Listen," she whispered, her accent coloring her words, "we stick to the truth. They have nothing on us."

"*Truth* feels flimsy right now, Sam," I hissed out, trying to keep my voice from being heard.

"Better than lies," she countered, her posture rigid against the seat, defiance etched into every line of her body.

"It's not like they're going to listen," I spat, the heat of my anger flushing my face. "They've already made up their minds."

"We were calling to turn ourselves in," Tom said, clenching his fists, struggling to push his fear down. "We stick to the plan."

But that was the kicker—the plan was unraveling before we'd had a chance. It would have been different if we'd come in on our own terms. Now, we were the criminals they'd caught red-handed. I adjusted in the back seat, trying to find an angle to see the thugs. They still sat watching, not a care in the world. The passenger door opened, and the other officer started climbing in.

Harris put up his hand. "I'll take these three myself," he barked at the officer, his silhouette blocking out the flickering neon of a sign across the street.

"Bit personal for you, isn't it, detective?" Yet the officer backed up anyway.

Harris reached across the cruiser and pulled the door shut.

The engine came to life, and we careened down the street, sirens wailing out their sad song. Road signs and storefronts streaked past us in blurs of color, reds, blues, yellows—all smearing past us in a continuous stream. The city was alive with sound and color, but inside that cop car, we were hurtling through a void with no idea what the next moment would bring.

There was no turning back now. I resigned myself to realizing this was the hand we were being dealt. Harris was trying to do his job, even if he was being a dick about it. We only had to do what Sam said and stick to the truth. We might have been cuffed and shoved into the back of a cop car, but we weren't proven guilty yet.

The police cruiser barreled through an intersection, red and blue flashing across the buildings in contrasting colors. My head was reeling, trying to come up with the right combination of words to convince Harris we didn't do this. The car skidded around another corner, tires screaming and leaving their mark for everyone to see. I caught Harris's grey eyes locked onto mine in the rearview. Nothing but a challenge in them. He thought he had us, thought the story was over.

I shifted in the cruiser's back seat to catch Harris's eye in the mirror again. "Listen," I started, my voice edged with tension. "You've got this wrong. We were up in Winnipeg when..."

"Save it," Harris cut me off, "I checked with border patrol. They have no record of you crossing. Convenient, huh?"

Tom's shook his head, disbelief etched into his features. "We went through," he insisted, defiance laced with fear. "That has to be a mistake."

"Quiet!" Harris barked, the word sharp like broken glass.

Sam sat, her jaw clenched, eyes fixed straight ahead. She'd rather throw a punch than argue, but she knew now wasn't the time. No matter how much she wanted to. I watched as her fists clenched and unclenched.

"Tell me about Charlie," Harris demanded, looking back at me. His voice sounded deeper all of a sudden.

"Charlie? He managed our gigs. He was our friend. Not much more to tell than that," I said, mustering as much cool as I could while cuffed in the back of a squad car.

"Cut the crap, Sticks. Where were you the night he died?" Harris's question spilled out of his mouth. He wanted to catch us in a lie.

"We were at a club in Winnipeg, then we drove back and crashed at our place. Woke up in this nightmare." I was sticking to the truth but stopping before we went and got an eyeful of our first dead body. Harris didn't need that bit of information yet.

"Convenient alibi. There are no witnesses other than the three of you. Like you would ever rat on each other," he retorted, skepticism seeping from every syllable.

"Man, if you think we killed Charlie, you've completely lost the thread." My anger was rising, my face turning red, and my ears felt like they were on fire.

"Right, three punk rockers and their dead manager. Nothing strange at all," Harris mocked, raising his eyebrows.

"Charlie might've been a little slimy, but he was our manager, our friend. He was working to book us bigger gigs. Why would we off the guy who was trying to help us?"

"Maybe it wasn't about the music," Harris mused, eyes narrowing. "Maybe there's more to your little band than meets the eye."

"Whatever you think we did or didn't do, we deserve a chance to clear our names," I stated, defiance flaring against fate's hand.

Harris didn't respond. He kept his eyes on the road, each turn taking us closer to the station and further from solving this. My mind raced, desperate to find a way out.

"Listen, Harris!" My raw and urgent voice clawed its way out. "We didn't have anything to do with Charlie. None of us did." Being crushed between my bandmates in the backseat of the cruiser was like a straitjacket—too tight, too confining. It was hard to breathe.

Harris's eyes flicked up to meet mine in the rearview, "Sure. Wrong place, wrong time, right? Save it. I've heard it all before."

"Damn it, you've got it all twisted!" I insisted, my words tumbling out, getting more desperate. "You've already convicted us. Let us explain."

"You'll have your chance," he said, a smirk playing at the corners of his mouth, his grip tightening on the steering wheel. "You'll have all the time you need to lay this out for us at the station."

I slumped back in the seat. It was useless. He wasn't listening to a word we had to say.

Tom's gaze flicked to me. No stage presence here, no puffed-up persona leading the song. He had shrunken down to take up as little space as possible. "Sticks," he murmured, "this is bad. Like the-end-of-the-line bad."

"It's not over yet," I said, trying to infuse some measure of authority into my voice.

Sam shifted next to me, her face turned downward. She held her hands clasped in her lap, breathing steady and even.

"You good, Sam?" I asked.

A quick nod in reply. That was all I was getting.

"It'll be fine," I assured. "We need to stick to the truth, and we'll be good."

"You realize the trouble you're in right now, don't you?" Harris asked from the front. Eyes shifting to the road, then back to the mirror to gauge my reaction.

"Once we can explain ourselves, you'll see we didn't do this," I said, hoping I could convince him.

Harris stared at me for a few moments. "You believe that, don't you?"

"Listen," I said, " I know you think we did this...'

"Enough, *Sticks*. Do you think this is a game?"

"Does it sound like I'm playing, Detective?" I screamed back, punching my fist into the divider between us, anger winning out over sense.

"Hey!" Harris barked, but I wasn't done—not even close.

"Charlie was family! You're pinning his death on us without a shred of real proof."

"Keep it up, and you'll be in solitary before you can count to four, drummer boy," he threatened, but it was just noise to me now.

"Then throw me in solitary!" I spat the words, the rage tumbling out of me. "But we won't stop fighting, not until the real murderer is in these cuffs."

Harris pulled the car into the front of the station. A squat brick building that resembled something a kid had built with Lego. A box meant to hold people inside—that was it. My stomach dropped as we came to a stop. Waiting outside were several reporters with cameras and microphones. Sam spotted it, too, and adjusted her hair to cover more of her face. Tom turned white.

"Cameras?" he said. "What's with the cameras?"

"Didn't you know?" Harris said, undoing his seatbelt and reaching to grab the handle. "You guys are famous."

He chuckled at his joke as he exited and opened the back door, getting each one of us out and leading us toward the station doors.

"Detective Harris!" one of the reporters shouted. "Is it true these three are related to The Palms murder?"

Harris shuffled us past, saying, "Can't comment on an ongoing investigation."

That sounded like a yes to me.

Sam stayed between Tom and me, her face down, not looking at the cameras. It made me a little jealous. I wanted nothing more in that moment than to not be seen. We ducked our heads and made our way inside the station, followed by the sounds of multiple people shouting questions and flashbulbs popping.

Harris closed the door behind us, shutting out the clamoring reporters. He cleared his throat and taunted, "Feel like rock stars yet?"

Chapter 16

Sunday, September 7th, 1986, 11:04 a.m.

"**Y**ou." A young officer behind the desk pointed at me. "Name?"

"Sticks...ah... Francis Marshall," I stumbled, realizing they probably weren't fans of nicknames here.

He sized me up, eyes as cold as the steel table he was leaning over and gesturing to the ink pad in front of him. One by one, he took my fingers and made prints on a white card with my name scrawled across the top. Each line of my fingerprint was captured like it was a written confession.

He waved me aside. "Your turn." He waved Tom up to the counter. "Name?"

"Tom Williams," Tom said. His mohawk showed signs of losing its eternal fight with gravity. The tips of it just barely drooped to one side. The officer repeated the steps with Tom and got his fingerprints on the card.

"Next." He gestured Sam forward. "Name?"

"Sam," she said.

"Full name?" The cop rolled his eyes, annoyed.

"Sam," she repeated. "Just Sam."

The cop shook his head in an "I don't get paid enough for this" fashion. After taking her prints, he dismissed Sam over to the rest of us.

Another officer grabbed me by the upper arm and directed me toward a wall hashed with black lines.

"Face the camera, please," a lanky cop barked, ushering us one by one in front of the height chart. Flash after flash, our mugshots snapped.

"Move it." They nudged us forward, shuffling down the corridor, the peeling paint on the walls revealing patches of old, discolored plaster. Doors clicked open, metal frames echoing our passage into the belly of this concrete beast.

Fear tightened its grip on me. One wrong move, and we'd never see outside this place again. No more sky. Bye-bye, freedom.

"Marshall, in here." A redheaded cop directed me into a cramped room—empty, save for a cold metal table, two chairs, and a framed mirror on one wall. Like in the movies, I pictured Harris standing on the other side of the glass, waiting for me to slip up and admit to the whole thing. Make his job easy. *You're out of luck, Harris. I'm still innocent.* I smiled at the mirror with what little defiance I could muster.

The door thumped shut, leaving me alone. My reflection in the two-way mirror was my only company. I slumped back in the chair; it was hard and unforgiving. I tried to prepare myself for what was coming. The ink on my fingers tightened on my skin as it dried, and the stale scent of fear seemed to seep out of every surface here. This place, this room, was meant to break you, peeling back your layers until nothing was left but the truth.

I stood up and paced around the room, nervous energy spilling out of me. The door cracked open, a slight hesitation, then the rest of the way in a smooth motion.

"Sit down, Marshall," Harris said, stepping inside. His gray eyes were already staring into me, daring me to step out of line.

I slumped back into the chair, its cold frame chilling me through my clothes.

Harris sat, fingers folded together like a silent prayer. I could imagine him saying, *God, please make this quick.*

"Back to the top," he demanded, not wasting any breath on pleasantries. "When was the last time you talked to Charlie Fitzpatrick?"

"Thursday, after our show in Winnipeg. We drove up crazy early that morning. Got ready, played, and then called him to check in."

"Did Charlie say anything to you when you called him?"

"He told us he'd gotten us another gig. We were excited about it."

Harris was taking everything down, scribbling in his little notebook, using a pen with a cap that had been chewed on more than it was used for its intended purpose.

Harris stopped writing. "Where was the job?

I braced myself. We'd decided on the truth, so here we went. "The Palms. It would have been our first time headlining at a real venue."

Harris did not react to the mention of The Palms. He made a quick note. "So, what did you do then?"

"We finished playing at Wellington's in Winnipeg, said our goodbyes to the bartender, Lena, and headed back right away."

"So, you drove through the night?"

"We did," I said, trying to make out what he was scratching in his notebook. He must have noticed because he slid back in his chair and moved the notebook to his lap. "We wanted some sleep before rehearsal that night."

"Anything eventful on the way home?" he asked, one eyebrow cocked at me.

"No, we spoke with the border guard, Liam. He usually waves us into his lane when he sees us. He's a friend of Charlie's."

The intensity of the notepad scribbling picked up for a couple of seconds. His writing slowed, then stopped. "So, uneventful trip home. It's now Friday morning, early. What then?"

"Straight home, crashed right away so we could rest up. Woke up in the afternoon almost late for rehearsal already." My words were starting to slow down. We were approaching what I didn't want to talk about.

"What next? It's now Friday afternoon."

"We made our way to The Palms to rehearse. When we walked in, it was quiet. There were no sound techs, no manager, no nothing."

"Unusual," Harris said but motioned me to go on. He was leaning forward now, anticipating this next bit as much as I was dreading it.

"We made our way around, looking for Charlie, but we didn't see him anywhere. We headed backstage and…" I stopped. It was getting harder to speak.

Harris, leaning forward, pushed a glass of water I hadn't noticed on the table over to me. "Take your time."

I picked it up and took a few swallows. It did nothing to distract me from the feeling creeping through every nerve in my body. "We opened the door and found Charlie. He was dead."

"So, when we met that first time, you already knew?" Harris was scribbling with fury now. It was shocking that his pen didn't snap in half.

"We did. We figured the blame would be put on us, so we decided to solve this thing ourselves."

"Like the Hardy Boys and Nancy Drew." Harris's face quirked a smile as he said it. "Did you see anything else? What made you run?"

"Well, the drumstick with my name on it seemed like a clear indicator that you would be coming after me." I was breathing shallowly at this point. A sort of numbness came over me. My body was taking the time to go into proper shock.

"Good guess. So, the drumstick had your name on it. Then what?" Harris was clinical about this.

"We checked around and found a bag on Charlie with this symbol." Time to lay out all our cards. I tossed the folded-up paper across the table to Harris.

He carefully unfolded it, gave it a once-over, and folded it back up without reacting. "So, you found the body of your friend. He had your drumstick in his eye and drugs on him. Do I have that right?"

"Yes. That covers it."

"So, instead of being smart and calling the cops, you decide to run out and be detectives? Running all over the city, guns going off, cars speeding through the streets. The crime rate has gone up about twenty-five percent since that night." Harris flipped through the notes he had been taking. "Why should I believe you?"

"It's the truth," I said. "I admit, we are way out of our depth. We wanted some proof that we didn't do it. We didn't think you'd believe us. Once Big Tony got wind we were sniffing around about that symbol, we were definitely in way too deep."

Harris stopped dead. "Big Tony?"

"Yeah, you gave us his name, he's a gangster from Chicago who moved into town. That snake thing is his mark."

"I *know* who Big Tony is," Harris interrupted. "You think he has something to do with Charlie's murder?" Harris was back at his notebook again.

"It sure seems likely to us. The drugs..." I started, but Harris waved me off before I could finish. He stood up and marched out of the room. The door clicked closed behind him.

My mind was racing. Harris wasn't buying it. I hadn't even told him about the drugs we'd found stashed in the tire yet.

Moments passed, then minutes. The doorknob turned, and Harris made his way back in. He was talking to someone behind him when he stopped halfway in the door.

"What do you want me to do about it? If she won't talk, she won't talk."

I smiled. Sam was being her usual charming self. Harris came the rest of the way in and sat down, leaving the other officer to deal with Sam. *Best of luck with that.*

"I just looked again. Nothing with the symbol on it was signed into evidence." Harris was watching me closely.

"I didn't have a chance to say. We took the baggie with us to use as evidence while we investigated ourselves."

Harris's face was growing redder by the moment. "You're idiots, every one of you. Even if I believed the bullshit you're telling me, you've tampered with evidence." Harris had started in a normal tone of voice, but by the end, he was yelling. "You're a punk band, not detectives. Even if you're innocent, you're in deep shit now."

I clenched my fists in my lap to stop them from shaking. "We were scared and wanted to prove we didn't do it," I said, never looking up.

"Well, you did a terrible job. You sit here for a while. I need to go check on your friends' stories. Well, Tom's story, in any case."

Harris got up and stormed out of the room. The door clicking shut behind him made me jump. It felt final, like the end of something. Our chance at freedom, maybe.

Time ticked by, dragging on for what felt like hours. The clock hung high on the wall, secured behind a metal cage, the only sound in the room. *Tick, tick, tick.* Each *tick* brought a flash of memory of everything we'd been through.

Tick. The show in Winnipeg.

Tick. Sam kicking the drunk guy off the stage.

Tick. Me pulling the homeless guy off the road.

Tick. Charlie's body.

Tick. Big Tony's men firing on us.

Tick. The hotel room blowing apart around us.

Tick. Harris with his gun pointed at us.

Click. The door opened. Another officer motioned for me to stand up, grabbing me by the arm as I did so. He led me down a long hallway and into a holding area. Tom and Sam already sat behind bars. There was only one other cell in the room and it was empty.

When they opened the door, it slid back with a loud clanging of metal on metal. The officer ushered me inside, sliding the door closed behind me and locking it in one smooth motion. He walked out without ever saying a word.

"Well, that was fun," Tom said from the bench in front of me, the magic of his mohawk had abandoned him. The top half was drooping to one side, and the rest was about ready to give up as well.

"How'd it go?" I asked Tom.

"I mean, it sucked. I told them everything that happened, stuck to the truth as much as possible."

"Same here," I said. "I never told them about the rest of the drugs we found, though. Never had the chance. They were focused on Charlie, not what came after."

"Ditto," Tom said. "Not sure if that's a good or bad thing."

"Me neither, but we've still got a card up our sleeve." I shrugged and turned to Sam. "I think I know how your conversation went."

Sam smiled a little. "They said I had the right to remain silent, so I did."

"So, what do we do now?" Tom asked.

"We wait," I answered. "Harris will come back in, and we'll be able to put our cards on the table and try to find a way out of this mess."

I was doing my best to be confident. Or at least *sound* confident. "We stick with Sam's idea. We can use the drugs as bait to draw Big Tony out, and they can bust the real killer."

It seemed that being arrested was not as exciting as it was in the movies. It was all questions and waiting—lots of waiting.

After an eternity of counting the minutes passing by, the door unlocked and swung open. We all stood up, getting ready to plead our case to Harris, to convince him we were innocent and help us take out Tony.

There was only one problem.

It wasn't Harris.

Chapter 17

Sunday, September 7th, 1986, 12:48 p.m.

"**W**ell, if it isn't the world-famous Bombs Away." I didn't recognize him. He was tall with a hawkish nose and a red face like his cheeks had been slapped.

Right behind him was his opposite. A short, potbellied man, pale and blond. Both were in uniform, both strutting in like they owned the place. They stopped before our cell, smirking at us through the bars.

Hawk Nose was talking again. "This is quite the predicament you've gotten yourselves into."

"We're waiting to talk to Harris." I backed away from the bars, not wanting to engage.

"Don't worry about Harris. You're not his problem," Potbelly said. "Now you're our problem." His hand rested on the revolver at his hip.

"We want to know more about your pal Charlie," Hawk Nose said.

"We already told Harris everything, but ask away."

These two made me uneasy from the moment they walked through the door. My friends were showing signs they felt the same way. Tom was staring at the floor, likely thinking that if he didn't make eye contact, the problem would go away. Sam was almost motionless, but she still seemed poised and ready to go off at any moment.

"Shame what happened to him," Potbelly mused. "You all have anything to do with that?"

"Charlie was our manager and our friend," I answered. "We didn't kill him. We already told Harris all of this."

"We're running this investigation now!" Hawk Nose snapped.

"Excuse my colleague here," Potbelly interrupted. "He gets a little tense about all this murder business. We were curious if you knew anything about the missing merchandise."

"Merchandise?" Tom questioned. "Like what? T-shirts and stuff?"

"No." Potbelly chuckled. "Not T-shirts. Something a little more expensive."

"It should be in our statement. We found a small bag of powder at the crime scene. That's it," I said, wondering what they were doing, asking us the same things over and over. The hairs on the back of my neck stood up.

"Right, right..." Hawk Nose said. "I feel like the three of you aren't telling us everything."

We knew this routine all too well. We'd seen it a million times on TV. Good cop, bad cop.

"How about we stop with this, and you tell us what you want," Sam said, narrowing her eyes and leaning back against the cold cell wall. "Stop pretending and ask."

Hawk Nose eyed Sam from top to bottom, his smirk spreading into a grin. "Tell us where the merchandise is, and we'll get outta here."

"We don't know what you're talking about," I said, hoping they couldn't see the lie written all over my face. I couldn't let them discover that our only leverage was sitting in another warehouse, minutes from where we lived.

"Big Tony wants his property back," Potbelly said. "The sooner that happens, the sooner this can all be over."

"We don't have his property," I lied. "What he can do is confess to killing Charlie, and we can all move on with our lives."

"That's not happening." Potbelly was done with *good cop*. Now we had *bad cop* and *worse cop*.

The cell felt stifling, as if the walls themselves were closing in like the suffocating press of fans at a sold-out show.

Hawk Nose leaned against the bars, tapping them with keys on a chain attached to his belt. "Listen, punks," he said, his voice carrying an unmistakable threat. "You're in deep, and it's only going to get deeper unless you start talking. We know you've got it. Tell us where it is."

"Nah, we don't have anything you want." I sat down and averted my gaze. "We'll wait on Harris."

"Look at me!" Hawk Nose screamed. "Harris can't save you now. Tony wants something you have and won't stop coming at you until he gets it."

"Round and round we go," I said. "How many times do you need to hear the same answer?"

"Once more. Right to my face." Hawk Nose moved right up to the cell door. He put the key in and turned. The cell door clanged open, echoing ominously in the small space.

Sam was already on her feet in a defensive position, hands up. Tom scrambled back into the corner, back to the wall, hands raised in fists in front of him. I stood my ground. Let him ask me. He was going to get the same answer.

"Last chance," Potbelly said, falling in behind his buddy. "The drugs or the grave."

They both had their hands on the revolvers at their hip and were approaching us.

A loud noise echoed through the room, and I jumped, thinking, *Gunshot!*

I turned toward the source and saw Harris standing at the door to the holding area, eyes on us. He'd opened the door with enough force to break some of the tiles on the wall.

"Back away," he called out. His weapon was already drawn and pointed at them. They froze in surprise—surprise, and fear.

"D... Detective," Hawk Nose stammered, his hand sliding away from his revolver. "We were just—"

"Stop," Harris cut him off, his gaze as cold as the steel bars between us. "This better be one hell of an excuse."

The balance of power flipped like a light switch. Harris now held everyone's attention.

"We were questioning them," Potbelly tried, voice slick as oil.

Harris's eyes narrowed at him. "Questioning my suspects? Why?"

"We thought we could pry some more out of them." Hawk Nose had his hands up in the air. "Just routine stuff."

"Routine?" Harris growled, his voice low and dangerous.

The officers exchanged glances, the wordless communication of rats caught in a trap. They knew the jig was up. The three of us watched from our cramped cell. After all the crap we'd been through these last few days, our luck was going to turn around. Harris might be the one cop not on Tony's payroll.

"Routine, my ass." Harris raised his revolver.

They opened their mouths to protest.

"Save it," Harris barked before they could speak. "You two have Big Tony's stink all over you." The detective took one hand off his weapon and signaled someone behind him.

A couple more men came in and looked to Harris for more instruction.

"I want cuffs on both. Take them to one of the interrogation rooms. I'll deal with it shortly."

Harris still had his aim trained on the cell. The other two who entered the room holstered their pistols and started taking out their cuffs.

In an instant, Potbelly had Tom around the neck with a gun to his head.

"You're gonna let us walk out of here," Potbelly said, the barrel steady against Tom's temple. "Back away!"

Harris had lowered his weapon but had not put it away. The two new cops who had entered the room had their hands up submissively, cuffs dangling from one hand.

Potbelly turned his head to Hawk Nose. "Come on! Grab her. Let's go."

Hawk Nose moved toward Sam with a smile on his face. His gun pointed at her stomach.

Sam, with a bored voice, asked Harris, "Are you going to do something about this?" Her one visible eyebrow arched.

Harris's mouth opened as if to say something, but Sam didn't wait. She took hold of the pistol in Hawk Nose's hand and twisted it back towards his body. In an instant, Sam was holding it in her hand. She swung it against the side of Hawk Nose's head, knocking him out cold. He slumped down on the floor with a long groan.

That familiar *click* sounded through the cell when Sam pulled the hammer back on the revolver and aimed it at Potbelly.

"Let. Him. Go," she stated while she pressed the barrel into the back of his head to punctuate each word.

Pot Belly lifted his hands, the revolver now dangling from one finger. Sam grabbed it and knocked him over the head, too. Before he even hit the ground, she was emptying the revolvers onto the concrete floor. She laid the guns on the bench and stepped away.

"All yours, Harris," she said with her palms up, backing further away.

Tom hugged her hard when she got close to him. "Thanks, Sam!" he said as he withdrew. He turned a dark shade of red as he realized his outburst. He straightened his shirt and shoved his hands into his pockets.

The three of us pressed against the back wall as far away from the unconscious men and their weapons as possible. Harris and his other two men made their way in. They grabbed the guns and the thugs and began moving them out of the room.

Harris kept looking from the unconscious cops to Sam and back again. "Someday, I'm going to want to know how you did that," he said to her, shaking his head.

"You've got some problems at your precinct if this," I began, gesturing at the two being carried away, "is how things will be. I take it they aren't friends of yours?"

"I've seen them around," he said, rubbing the stubble on his jaw. "They were newer. Only on the force for a year or so."

"You think they were the only ones Big Tony got to? Or are we sitting ducks in here?" I asked, but I already knew the answer.

"I..." Harris started but hesitated. "I don't know anymore. If you asked me that question an hour ago, I knew you three were guilty. Now, I have no idea."

"Big Tony and his crew are a cancer in this town," I said, with a deep scowl. "Everywhere we've gone, he's been tracking us. Old friends, hotel managers. He's been one step ahead of us the whole time."

"Why is he after you?" Harris asked. "It has to do with Charlie?"

"It's the last bit of the puzzle we haven't been able to tell you yet," I said, nodding eagerly as I moved away from the wall. "We found the drugs on Charlie and started investigating. We showed the symbol we found to figure out who was behind it all, which led us to Tony. The only problem is, we didn't realize he was already looking for us, too."

Harris sat down on the bench in the cell. His weapon holstered again, but he kept stealing looks at the door and watching, just in case.

"After we did some digging," I continued, "we found out Charlie and Big Tony had been using our shows in Winnipeg as cover."

"Drugs?" Harris asked.

"Yeah, hidden in the spare tire of our van. We'd been smuggling pounds of cocaine across the border. We had no idea, and I have no idea for how long, maybe right from the start."

"So, you've got his stuff?" Harris said, connecting the dots.

"We found the latest haul and stashed it before you brought us in. Your buddies were asking us where it was right before you came in." It was a welcome change to tell the whole truth for once. "Our theory is Charlie got mixed up in it. Big Tony wasn't happy for some reason, and they took him out."

A gunshot rang out, muffled by the closed door to the holding cells but still causing all of us to flinch and duck.

Harris flew into action and bolted out of the room, leaving the cell door unlocked and open as he did.

I turned to Sam and Tom. Tom's eyes were darting around, looking for any sign of danger. Through the door, people shouting, more gunshots ringing out. Then silence.

"I'm staying here," Tom said, sitting on the bench again and crossing his arms.

Sam sat next to him, her hands threaded together in her lap. Her eyes found me as she said, "Let's hope there are more good cops than bad ones out there."

The silence grew oppressive. We strained our ears to try to make out anything beyond the door. We heard the occasional shuffle of someone walking and a faint shout we couldn't make out the words to.

The minutes stretched way too long. I paced in the cell, drumming out beats with my hands as I ran them along the bars. The door slammed open, bashing into the broken tiles on the wall again.

Sam jumped to her feet, fists up and ready. Tom stood behind her, peeking at the door from behind her shoulder. I backed away from the bars as we watched the figure enter the room.

Harris's voice called out to us as he stepped in further. "Well, if I was still convinced you were guilty, I would question it now." He smiled easily, in a very good mood for how bad this day had turned out. "Cell door wide open, and you're all still sitting here. You're either very innocent or very stupid."

Harris took in the three of us, then around the room like he was seeing it for the first time. "Let's go somewhere less 'jail' to figure all this out."

Chapter 18

Sunday, September 7th, 1986, 1:10 p.m.

Harris waved to us with a "come on already" motion. The three of us glanced at each other and then made our way down the halls of the police station. I was afraid if we didn't move quickly, he'd change his mind and take us back to our cell. We all stood together near the lobby. Harris turned to look us over like he was seeing us for the first time.

"Yeah, you all are inconspicuous as hell," he said, raising one eyebrow. "Stay close to me, and try not to draw any attention to yourselves."

Harris turned to leave, and we shuffled in behind him, keeping our heads down. There wasn't much we could do, we were about as incognito as three punks in a police station could get. Tom stuck close to Harris, hiding behind his larger frame. His head swiveling back and forth, looking for trouble but also, he seemed excited at the prospect of getting the hell out of this place. Sam strolled along like she belonged here. If I didn't know better, she acted like she had been confident we would walk out of there the whole time.

We rounded the corner into chaos. A few ambulances were visible through the front windows, back doors wide open. The wounded had paramedics around, treating them for various injuries. Papers littered the desks and floors like a bomb had gone off.

I glanced around and saw several bullet holes decorating the walls. I realized I was gawking like a tourist, so I stopped craning my neck to check out every corner. My eyes went to the floor, and instead of linoleum, I saw body bags—two of them occupied and zipped up.

Shuffling around Tom, I tapped Harris on the back. Leaning in I whispered, "Were your guys seriously hurt?"

"Only those two that came after you. They grabbed a gun off someone's belt and tried to run off again. They didn't last long. Only a couple of close calls on our side."

He led us into an empty office, far away from all the commotion of the station floor. It was barren except for a metal table and a couple of chairs that, like us, had seen better days. Fluorescent tubes flickered and buzzed in the water-stained drop ceiling above us. The room was sparse and cold, but it still felt like freedom. There were no bars, locks, or toilet in the corner. That was always a plus when you were in any room that wasn't a bathroom.

Harris grunted as he fell into one of the metal chairs. I realized he was favoring one of his legs.

"You gonna make it?" I asked him.

"Bullet grazed my leg," he said calmly, like this happened all the time, just some gunplay around the office. He stared us down with an unreadable gaze. "Spill it."

"We know Big Tony is behind all this." I walked around the table and fell into the other chair. "He wouldn't be after us so hard if we weren't onto something. He wants his product and wants us to stop asking questions about Charlie. "

Harris nodded. "I figured that much out when two of my fellow *officers* tried to take you out in broad daylight."

"When we started digging into this," I went on, "they were onto us really quick. We holed up with a friend, who ended up turning on us."

"Name?" Harris asked, his little notebook appearing almost instantly. Harris's well-practiced magic trick.

"Mick... Michael Jenkins." I stumbled with his full name. I'd never called him Michael. "We heard him on the phone, and he mentioned not knowing where our van was. Since we didn't get why they'd care about our old junker, we checked it out and found a whole bunch of drugs stashed in it."

"Yeah, you mentioned that. How much is a whole bunch?" Harris asked.

"We didn't take the time to weigh it," I said, "but based on the size of the bags, about eight kilos. We hid it and took off."

Harris whistled, then said, "No wonder he's pissed. I wish you had come clean earlier."

"Can you say," Sam interjected, "that you would have given us a chance to explain if you'd found us at the crime scene near a murder weapon with Stick's name on it?"

"I..." Harris trailed off when he saw Sam's dead-eyed stare and paused. "Probably not."

"With Big Tony running everything the way he is," I said, holding my index finger in the air for emphasis, "there's only one way we're going to take him out."

"How's that?" Harris asked leaning forward, the chair creaking in protest. Harris groaned a little and held his leg.

"We give him what he wants. We offer ourselves and the dope. When he comes, we keep him talking, and you do your thing and put him away."

"This isn't the movies, kid." Harris was shaking his head as he said it. "You need to leave this up to us."

"What evidence do you have on Big Tony right now?" I asked, even though I knew the answer.

Harris paused like he wanted to say something but never did.

"Nothing, right? I'm assuming those two that came after us didn't run around shooting and saying, 'Big Tony made us do it.'"

Harris narrowed his eyes at me. I didn't think he "liked my tone," as my father used to say.

"It's way too dangerous," Harris countered, leaning back in his chair, his voice tinged with apprehension.

"I'm sorry," Tom said, "but if we leave it alone and let you gather evidence over time, we'll be dead long before you find enough. Nothing has been tied to him yet, or you'd already have put him away. We need to bring him out where we can make him talk, make him fess up to everything."

Harris was listening, at least. He sat, arms crossed like a sullen teenager, weighing his options. For a cop, he sure didn't have much of a poker face. His emotions were plain as day, written across his features while he worked through all the possibilities. I kept talking, hoping I could make him see our reasoning.

"We don't want to do this, but using ourselves as bait is the only way we can lure him out of hiding." I stared Harris right in the eyes. "He won't suspect us, not now. He thinks we're scared, broken, and on the run. We'll tell him we escaped when his men attacked here, and we slipped out in the chaos."

Harris sat with his hand on his chin, mulling it over, so I continued, "We tell him we want it to end. We should be able to sell that. It's the truth."

"What makes you think he'll even come himself?"

"Well," I considered, "he wants his drugs for one thing, but, at this point, he probably just wants to kill us himself. We've been a serious thorn in his side these last couple days. Also, I don't think he's a fan of our band."

Harris's face went through several more emotions. Finally, he let out a long sigh. "Damn it." Another groan got him out of the chair. "You've got guts. I'll give you that much. The jury's still out on the brains. If your plan works..."

"It will work," I assured him, the determination of my bandmates radiating beside me. "It has to."

"Even if it kills us," Tom added, sounding far more confident than usual. The only tell was the nervous gulp of a swallow he took.

Harris paced around the room. He was still thinking it over. His eyes were mainly on the floor, but he sometimes looked up to take us in, sizing us up for the task at hand. He ran his hand through what was left on top of his head. A few wisps were trying to run away. He caught them and smoothed them back down along with the rest.

His pacing slowed down, then stopped. "Fine," He conceded, a reluctant ally drawn into our mad scheme. "We do this my way, though. We need to be controlled and calculated. We ensure we gather the evidence we need, evidence that can be used. Understood?"

"Understood," we echoed.

"You better understand. Or this could go sideways real fast," Harris said seriously, then a half-smile threatened to break through his stoic facade. "Now let's catch ourselves a bad guy."

Harris pivoted on his heel and walked out of the room. He hadn't motioned for us to follow, so we stayed put. We sat around the table. I had nothing but pure certainty that this was going to work. Now that everything was in motion, the nerves were setting in. Tom was fidgeting with his buttons and zippers. Sam sat in one of the chairs, head slightly bowed.

Harris re-entered the room carrying a cardboard box. He tossed it on the table next to us, turned, and left.

The room became a flurry of motion after that. Harris had found a few men he trusted who weren't nursing any wounds, and they started gathering everything we'd need for our sting operation.

Piles of equipment grew in the room around us: guns, ammo, listening devices, tape decks, and bullet-proof vests. We helped where we could, packing things into duffel bags. If there was one thing a band knew how to do, it was wrap cables.

No one other than Harris and his select few officers seemed to take notice of us or the room we were in. It was easy to avoid prying eyes with the mess Tony's crooked cops had made.

When Harris had gathered all the equipment he needed, the commotion died down. It was standing room only with the three of us, Harris, and the four officers he'd found—eight of us against Big Tony and whatever firepower he brought with him.

"Okay," Harris said, standing in the front with all eyes on him. He pointed to me. "Sticks here will be wired up. He will call one of Big Tony's known clubs from a nearby payphone and tell them he wants Big Tony to meet at the abandoned warehouse alone. We expect he'll ignore that last part. When he shows up, Sticks will get him to admit to the drugs and the mur-der. The minute we hear a confession or the codeword, we swoop in."

"He makes it sound so easy," Tom said under his breath.

One of the uniforms put his hand in the air. "What's the codeword?"

"Sticks?" Harris asked me.

"Backbeat," I said.

Tom threw the horns at me across the table. Rock and roll.

"You got that?" Harris said, scrutinizing all the faces around him. "Backbeat. Then we arrest the big man and anyone he brought with him. Everyone copy that?"

The whole room nodded in agreement. This was it. There was no turning back. One way or another, this was over today.

Tom spoke up. "So, how do we sneak out of here?"

"I have a plan," Harris answered. "We're going to make a commotion on the other side of the precinct. When you hear it, you go out the door and turn left. End of the hall, out the door. A black van will be waiting for you."

"We don't exactly blend in," I pointed out.

"That's why you'll be wearing these." Harris tossed three blue uniforms at us.

"My dad would be so proud." Tom's words dripped with sarcasm. "A man in uniform."

Harris and his men grabbed the duffel bags and equipment. The three of us got changed. Tom tucked his hair into his hat. Sam did a makeshift ponytail and somehow was the spitting image of an actual cop. I put the last uniform on, and it was about two sizes bigger than it needed to be. I rolled up my sleeves and pant legs like a kid dressed in his dad's clothes.

We waited by the door. The station had calmed down. The paramedics had left, and everyone was trying to pick up the pieces.

All of a sudden, Harris's voice was screaming, "They're gone! Where the hell are my prisoners?"

Another one of Harris's trusted cops yelled, "This way!"

I could hear dozens of footsteps receding as everyone hurried to the other end of the station to look for us. We cut out the door, down the hall, out into the waiting vehicle, slamming the door shut behind us the minute we were inside.

We huddled in the back, listening for signs that this didn't work. Long moments passed, but the driver's door swung open, and Harris fell into the seat.

"You better be right," he said. "I just risked everything for you three."

"We are," I assured him. "Everything go okay?"

"If Big Tony had any other cops on the payroll, they think you escaped." Harris didn't sound pleased at the thought of more crooked cops, but that was not today's problem. "Ready?"

"Rock and roll." I threw the horns at Harris.

Harris shook his head in the rearview mirror as if to say, "You're an idiot," but his eyes twinkled. He was enjoying this. Harris had a little punk rock in him after all. He cranked the van's engine and pulled out of the precinct parking lot on our way to what could be our last gig.

Chapter 19

Sunday, September 7th, 1986, 2:30 p.m.

A knot formed in my stomach when Harris said from the front, "We're here."

I exited the cramped back seat and took in the rusty, broken-down warehouse, all sheet metal and torn tar paper flapping in the wind. Not a glamorous place for a last stand, but it wasn't like we had a choice in the matter.

We unloaded our van along with a second one driven by the rest of Harris's team. A couple of the officers then drove both vans somewhere to stash them so they wouldn't be seen. I placed my box next to the others in the growing pile.

We only spent a few minutes here the last time. We hid the drugs and ran for it. The air reeked of metal and dust. Beams of sunlight cut across the interior at odd angles, breaking in through the rotten holes in the roof. Tom and Sam joined me and put their boxes down, looking around at the state of the place.

"What a dump," Tom said, his hands shoved deep into his pockets.

Harris approached us, grumbling about his leg all the while. "Let's get you wired up." He reached into the box and pulled out some tape and a wire. "Lift your shirt."

I followed orders, numb from what was about to happen. Harris taped the microphone on my chest and plugged it into a battery box, which he clipped near the small of my back.

"This doesn't have a huge range but should do the job," Harris said while he double checked the transmitter. "We'll be recording everything."

Harris stepped back, appraising me and giving me a firm pat on the shoulder. "All done. Remember, we need evidence. Concrete proof. You need to get him talking."

I pulled at my shirt, self-conscious that the microphone was visible. We'd changed back into our regular clothes on the drive over. They were ripe and could have used a wash. All I had was a T-shirt, so one of the policemen threw me a jacket. *Members only*. Not exactly my style. I felt like an idiot, but at least it covered the bulge of the microphone at my back.

"Well, let's hope Tony is feeling chatty today," I quipped. Behind my mask of confidence, my guts churned like a washing machine full of nails. I would have been a lot more comfortable with my drum set between me and the world.

"Here." Harris slipped a crumpled piece of paper into my hand. The phone number on it was harmless enough, numbers in black ink. It was more than that; it was a direct line to Big Tony's world. Harris had tracked down a number to one of his known hangouts. "Make the call, set the meet, then hustle your ass back here."

"Got it, boss," I said, giving Harris a terrible mock salute.

"Be careful, Sticks," Tom whispered, barely audible over the din of our preparations.

I clapped Tom and Sam on their backs in what I hoped was a reassuring way. "See you in a minute."

We were ready, a motley crew armed with the courage of desperation, the kind that came when you had nothing left to lose. Big Tony was about to get my call somewhere out in the city. He didn't realize it yet, but a clueless punk band was about to try and beat him at his own game.

I made my way to the door, adjusting the battery pack on the microphone as I went. I stepped out, and the second my boots hit the cracked pavement outside, everything sharpened. There was a slight chill in the air with the approaching fall weather, mixed with the overpowering smell of trash coming from the nearby dumpster. My pulse thudded like a bass drum. Every thump punctuated my steps while I left the warehouse. Nothing but the looming walls of the buildings around me and the distant screech of tires and honking of horns to keep me company.

I reached up and popped my stupid jacket's collar against the wind. I made a beeline for the pay phone. It stood alone, a sentinel at the corner. Chipped paint and worn buttons were its armor. The receiver was cold in my palm.

"Bombs Away..." I muttered to no one, punching in the numbers Harris had given me.

The receiver played the tones back to me as I dialed, discordant notes that set my teeth on edge. The line clicked a couple of times, rang only once, then connected.

"Yeah?" The gravelly voice on the other end of the line was more of a grunt than a greeting.

"I need to talk to Tony," I said, forcing my voice to be steady through my jitters.

"Who the hell is this?" Suspicion dripped from each word like oil.

"Tell Tony to get on the phone. I've got his stuff, and he's going to want to talk to me. Tell him it's Sticks." My grip on the receiver tightened. I wanted to say it was the strength of my will that had me holding it so tight, but I was scared it would slip out of my sweaty hand.

Another grunt-like acknowledgment came from the other end, and the receiver thudded on a table as it was set down without care. The *Jeopardy* theme played in my head as the minutes stretched on.

Finally, the receiver was picked up again—a deep, booming voice with a thick Chicago accent.

"Sticks," Tony said. "I heard you got pinched."

"You know we did. Your pet cops tried to kill us." I wasn't pulling punches.

"I'm hurt," Tony said, his voice pitched to feign innocence. "I never told anyone to do any such thing."

"Listen, you know they got popped. We got out in the commotion." I tried to keep my voice as calm as possible. "We want this over with. We've got your stuff, and we want a clean slate, no strings. You come alone and meet us at the warehouse on Harbour and Bay in one hour."

"Alone, huh? Why would I do that?"

"Because, *Tony*..." I let his name hang between us. "If we see otherwise, we might torch it all before you come in the door."

I doubted he bought my bluff, but I slammed the receiver down, preempting any argument or protest and trying my best to sell it. I sighed and turned to walk back to everyone. The clock was ticking now.

"Showtime," I called out as I entered the building.

Harris and his boys had put the coke in a neatly stacked pile under a hole in the ceiling. The afternoon sunlight shone like a spotlight down on it.

"One hour," Harris called out to his men. "Everyone in position. Make sure you're well hidden from all angles, and stay sharp. No mistakes today."

Harris's gaze swept over the dust-filled space, taking in every nook that could serve as a hideout for his team. As they positioned themselves with military precision, I watched silent as the phantoms slipped away into the shadows. They were nowhere to be seen from the center near the pile of Tony's goods where we stood.

Sam and Tom stood together like always on either side of me. "I'm sorry," I said, frowning as I wrung my hands together.

"Sorry for what?" Sam asked.

"All of this," I said, gesturing to everything around me. "The minute I thought about leaving the band, everything fell apart."

"This is not your fault," she said.

"I know that, I do, but I never should have even been thinking that. You're my family. I'm sorry I almost blew it."

"I, for one"—Tom was already smiling—"may never forgive you. I think you'll need to keep drumming with us forever to make up for it."

"Deal," I said, pulling them into a hug.

"This is so touching," Harris said from behind us. "But if you screw up my microphone, I'm gonna be pissed."

Tom and Sam stepped back from me while Harris fussed with the transmitter, making sure it was still all plugged in and working properly. He rearranged my newly acquired jacket and inspected me again, nodding in a "close enough" gesture.

"Big Tony will walk right into our trap." Harris was speaking to me now, straightening my collar. "Remember, tonight, you're not a drummer. You're a negotiator. You need to get him talking and keep him talking."

I nodded along, a little numb. The closer it got, the more real it all became. Some scary drug lord was about to stroll in here with his men armed to the teeth. They'd have no issues shooting me.

Harris grabbed my lapels and gave me a little shake. "Keep cool, Sticks. You've got this. Ask him questions, lots of questions. He'll lay it all out for you. When he does, we'll swoop in, and with any luck, he'll go away forever."

I nodded, the weight of the mic under my shirt getting heavier by the moment. I imagined it like a noose ready to tighten if I slipped up.

"Remember, we're right behind you," Harris reassured.

"And we're beside you," Sam said, putting her hand on my shoulder.

"I'll be beside you as well, but if shit goes down, I'm going to stand behind Sam," Tom said with a chuckle in his voice.

"You all should have no issues with this. Play your parts. You're performing. The spotlight is on you," Harris said. He disappeared into a group of old crates. As he did, he sang out, "And a one and a two…" with a mocking wave of his hands like an orchestra conductor.

The three of us huddled under the beam of light descending on center of the room, lighting the drugs up with a glow so bright I could still see their outline after looking away. It was silent, like the anticipation before a show; the tension in the audience as they waited for the first note to drop.

Tom echoed my thoughts. "It's just like waiting back-stage." His fingers fidgeted, trying to find something to do.

"Terrible crowd tonight, though," Sam remarked.

"Who needs a crowd when you've got company like this?" I said, smiling at my friends.

Almost exactly an hour after my call, the growl of an engine cut through the stillness. It circled the warehouse like a beast stalking its prey, pulled around by the door, and went quiet.

"Here we go," I breathed, my pulse thundering.

The concrete floor beneath our feet became a cold drum, echoing the thuds of closing car doors. Each door sent a message. One, two, three, four. Big Tony did not come alone. He was calling our bluff.

I nodded to my friends. Their grim and determined faces met mine. We were as ready as we could be. We'd do this together, no matter how tough it was. We would bring down the house.

Footsteps, heavy and deliberate, began to pound a rhythm into the ground. Each step resonated in the vast emptiness around us, growing louder as the unseen group approached the entrance.

"Stay sharp," I whispered, cracking my neck and rolling my shoulders to release some tension. I sucked in more of the stale air, trying to steady myself for what was about to happen.

A moment passed, then two. The door slid open with a bang. Standing in the beam of light made distinguishing details a little trickier. I saw their silhouettes start approaching. The footfalls counted their way to me. Dust stirred up with every movement, little clouds sparking in the light.

As they strode towards us, I saw a massive man in the middle and two others with him. There were only three. It was definitely four car doors that shut. If there was one thing I could say about myself, it was that I never missed a beat.

Let's hope that Harris's men can count to four like any drummer worth his salt.

Chapter 20

Sunday, September 7th, 1986, 3:46 p.m.

Everything hung suspended like the moment between a flash of lightning and the rumble of thunder—only the tapping of expensive shoes on ancient concrete counted the seconds. Big Tony stepped out of the shadows. His massive hulking form was like coming face to face with a force of nature, an avalanche in a business suit.

"The famous Bombs Away." I recognized the accent from the phone. "We finally meet in person. I see you've arranged everything in a neat little pile for me."

"Big Tony. It's nice to put a face to the name," I said, scanning him. Short-cropped curly hair hugged his head, and a bushy Brillo pad of a beard covered most of his face. The rest was pockmarked with acne scars and a bulbous nose that took up a good deal of real estate. "So happy to see you came alone as requested."

"I needed someone to carry all this product. I knew you'd never burn it. You're not that stupid," he said, inclining his head at the pile. The muscles under his suit flexed as we spoke. He could have carried the drugs and the tire they were smuggled in under one arm.

"I heard four doors slam," Tom said, ignoring his blatant lies. "Where's your other friend?"

"Well, aren't you three the little detectives that could?" Tony chuckled. The sound held no humor, only the dark promise of trouble. "He's making sure we're alone."

A wave of panic seized me, and my mind went to Harris and his men. *Let's hope they know how to play hide-and-seek.*

"We need to talk, Tony," I said, staring him dead in the eyes. It felt like he was seven feet tall.

"Do we now?" He raised his eyebrows. "About what, exactly?"

"Why did you kill Charlie?" I demanded, done dancing around this. I wanted answers.

"Charlie? I didn't kill Charlie. Word on the street is you did." His eyes were cold, his lips pressed into a thin line, not a hint of a smile crossing his face.

"We didn't kill Charlie. He was our friend. We found your stuff on him."

"You got me all wrong. Charlie worked for me, so I guess you could say you also worked for me." He was smirking now. "Charlie and me, we had a deal."

"What deal was that?" Tom asked.

"When I met Charlie, he was in deep. I helped get him out of the hole he dug himself into. So, he returned the favor by helping me bring my product into the country."

"Your *product*. You mean your *cocaine*," I said, my mind going to the uncomfortable box in my back transmitting all this.

"If you want to be crass about it, sure," Tony said. "My coke. He would have a group go up to Winnipeg, grab the drugs, and bring them back into the country. Then we'd pick them up and distribute them."

"Why us?" I asked, gesturing to my friends on either side of me.

"Not my department." Tony shrugged. "Charlie handled the details. It was my understanding he had friends in Winnipeg who would do the swap and friends at the border, so there would be no inspections at the crossing."

"Liam was in on this too?" I couldn't believe it, but it made sense.

"I have no idea who the fuck Liam is," Tony said. I could tell he was being honest. About this, at least.

"Charlie handled the details," I said, "so why kill him?"

"Like I said, I didn't kill Charlie. If one of you three didn't, I'm as stumped as you are." His voice was steady, but his eyes glinted with a hint of amusement.

I didn't believe a word he was saying.

"So, can I take my product now?" Tony asked. "Or are we going to stand around yapping all day?"

Tony's men advanced toward the pile. I stepped in front of them.

"We're not done here," I said. "I don't believe you about Charlie."

I was halfway through saying the word *believe* when I had two guns in my face. His men had drawn before I was even able to blink.

"I don't give a rat's ass what you believe," Tony gritted out, his voice pitched down, menacing. "You're going to get out of our way. I'm going to take my cocaine back, and you're going to be lucky if you're still alive."

Sam was tensed up next to me, like a snake ready to strike. I held out my hand to her, and she relaxed. Tom was not shrinking away. He was standing shoulder to shoulder with me, not moving. We looked at each other and nodded. In this together, then.

"We want answers about Charlie," I said again.

"Well, you're not gettin' them from me. I don't have any answers for you. Now move the fuck *out of my way!*"

The minute Tony started screaming, his men put thumbs on their pistols' hammers and pulled them back. They made a resounding *click*, the guns rising toward mine and Tom's faces.

Before they could raise them all the way, the world exploded with sound. Two loud pops, and Tony's men were on the ground—holes directly between their eyes.

Oh, well. Who needed a codeword anyway?

Tom retched to the right of me. I took a step back. Sam stepped up to my left, and Tom, wiping his mouth, stood back up. Standing together side by side, facing down Tony. He didn't seem as tall anymore.

"You... what..." Tony's head swiveled around, confused.

Tony's fourth man busted in through the door, racing to his boss. His pistol was already pointed at us—

Another cacophony and a flash of light. I was shoved to the side right into Sam. We both tumbled to the ground, not knowing what was happening.

Another blast, and Tony's man was on the ground, as still as the first two. I got up to my knees and tried to find my bearings.

Tom lay in a pool of blood.

"Tom!" I screamed out and scrambled on my hands and knees over to him. "Tom!"

He groaned on the ground and rolled over to face me, holding his shoulder. Sam raced up beside me and pressed her hands into his wound.

"Oooowwwwwww!" Tom moaned when she applied pressure.

"Be quiet, you stupid, brave idiot," Sam told him.

He smiled up at her, eyes unable to focus and delirious.

"Hi, Sam," he said, slurring. "He was gonna shoot you."

"I know," Sam said.

A metallic *click* behind me. Was it wrong that I was getting used to that sound?

"What a lovely scene," Tony said, grabbing me by my collar and hoisting me to my feet. "But we're leaving." I felt the cold barrel of his weapon as he pressed it into my temple. "I'm not sure who you've got shooting at me, but they can't kill me quick enough. You'll die too. Blondie," he said to Sam, "get my coke in the duffel and hand it to me."

Sam hesitated; her hands covered in Tom's blood.

"Your friend can bleed to death for all I care. Do it now, or both of your bandmates will be dead."

Sam let go of Tom's shoulder and made her way to the pile. Slowly, deliberately, she placed each brick into our ancient bag. Tony looked around the room, wild-eyed, constantly changing positions. He tried to keep me between him and all the weapons he knew were pointed at him. With his gun digging into my head, I couldn't even remember the codeword.

"Come on!" Big Tony screamed at Sam. "Let's go, let's go!"

Sam placed the last white brick into the duffel and picked it up. Before she stood up, I saw a glint of metal disappear back into her boot.

Tony pushed the barrel against the side of my head. "Don't move," he said through his teeth. "You, give me the stuff." He gestured to Sam with his free hand.

Sam came over and placed the straps into Tony's hand.

"Back away now. Slow." Tony momentarily shifted his aim from me to Sam. "I've been hearing about you. Some sort of kung fu chick."

Sam held her hands up and backed away. She gave me a slight nod and glanced at the duffel bag. Tony and I backed our way to the exit. Tony's eyes were still searching for whoever was watching.

"Don't do anything stupid," he called out. "I will leave with my product, and then Sticks here can go free. I promise."

Bullshit.

When we reached the door, he tapped my head with the base of his revolver in a "knock, knock" rhythm. "Open it up, drummer boy."

As I reached out to open the door, I swung it back far enough that Tony had to shift out of the way. When he did, he moved the bag enough to jostle the eight kilos inside.

When I heard the canvas ripping, I knew what Sam had done. Silently, she must have cut around the straps with the knife she kept in her boot. "A woman can't be too careful," she'd once said.

There was a loud tearing sound, and the tattered old material of the bag fell the rest of the way apart. The powder bricks fell out, thudding onto the floor at Tony's feet.

"Son of a bitch..." Tony cursed and started to bend down, reaching for the drugs.

The minute he did, I bolted.

To the left of the door were some old crates stacked up with a tarp thrown over them. I leaped over the lowest one and ducked behind it. I peeked over the top. Tony was kneeling, gun on the floor at his feet, trying to pick up whatever he could carry. He'd forgotten about me. He had four of five bricks in his arms. He stood and turned to face down the barrel of Harris's gun. The detective held his badge out like a shield beside it.

"Anthony O'Malley, you're under arrest for possession of narcotics with the intent to distribute, as well as for suspicion of murder in the case of Charles Fitzpatrick. Oh, and the attempted murder of Tom over there, and kidnapping, and a whole lot of other stuff. I've got a list. I'll let you look at it later."

Did Harris just tell a joke? Someone needed to check the temperature in hell. I think there's a cold front coming.

Big Tony paused for a moment before tossing all the drugs into the detective's face. He turned to run and got about three steps before he ran into Sam's outstretched arm.

Tony went down like a sack of potatoes as Sam clotheslined him, like a WWF wrestling match.

Harris hurried over and flipped Tony onto his stomach, handcuffing his giant arms behind his back. He sized up Tony and then Sam, who had taken just down a three-hundred-pound man with one arm.

"You're scary, girl," Harris said with a grin.

Sam smiled back at him and shrugged. She gave a mock curtsy and said with a deadpan stare, "Don't call me *girl*." She turned on her heel and ran over to Tom's side, pressing her hands back into his shoulder again.

"Owwwwwwwwww," Tom groaned. There wasn't much more blood than before, so they must not have hit anything too major.

Harris turned back to Tony and began to read him the rest of his rights. Two of Harris's men came out of the shadows to each hold one of Tony's arms.

Sirens in the distance got louder; the cavalry was on its way. Soon, red and blue lights flashed through windows, illuminating the concrete and rusty walls like a bad disco bar. Tony was escorted through the door to meet his fate.

I made my way over to Tom lying on the floor. "Hey, man, you saved my ass," I said, patting him on the good shoulder.

His eyes found mine, but they were glassy and unfocused. "Had to, it's too hard to find a decent drummer in this town."

He turned his attention back to Sam. He opened his mouth like he was about to say something, then passed out. His chest rose and fell.

Sam turned to me. "He's going to be fine. They need to dig this bullet out of his shoulder, and he'll be alright." I wasn't sure if she was trying to convince me or herself.

Harris came up behind us with some men. They loaded Tom onto a stretcher and took him out to a waiting ambulance.

Harris talked with us along the way. "You did great. We got everything we needed to put him away for a long time."

"He didn't admit to killing Charlie," I reminded, the anger rising in my voice.

Harris clapped me on the shoulder. "He will. It's a matter of time. We've got him now, and he's not going anywhere."

I sat on the ground next to Sam while a flurry of activity started around us. The crime scene was marked and photographed. Yellow numbers were placed around each body and the shells on the ground. An officer came over and took the wire equipment off me.

We were taken out to the ambulance, where Tom's shoulder was already being wrapped up. The paramedic was finishing it right as we approached.

"Just about all set here. Bullet hardly went in. He's lucky it didn't hit him a little to the right."

"Yeah?" Tom said, his words slurring. "You hear that? I'm lucky."

"He's also on a lot of painkillers," the paramedic said.

Harris joined us by the ambulance. He looked tired but happy. I tried to remember if I had ever seen him look this happy before. "Once they check out Tom a little more, we'll all go to the station and finish this mess. It's almost over."

I couldn't wait to be done with it all, but it didn't feel like a victory. Not yet. I wanted Tony's confession. We needed justice for Charlie.

Chapter 21

Sunday, September 7th, 1986, 9:02 p.m.

With the now familiar buzz of the station's fluorescent lighting, we sat three in a row on one side of the metal table in the interrogation room. At least we weren't in cuffs.

Tom's one arm was in a sling, free hand drumming on the table. He stopped and ran his hand through his bright blue hair, now hanging limp. "Man, this is killing me," Tom muttered. The slur of painkillers was gone.

Sam sat beside him, her hands in her lap. Her expression was calm and relaxed, she was taking deep slow breaths; the poster child for Zen and punk rock.

"We'll be okay, Tom," I tried to reassure him. "We're not under arrest this time. Harris needs to finish some paperwork, that's all."

We'd been sitting here at the station for several hours, answering more questions and reviewing all the details of what happened. He'd assured us we were almost finished—two hours ago.

The door to the interrogation room creaked open like part of some spooky soundtrack. Detective Harris stepped through the door, glancing behind him. All business, he directed a couple of unseen co-workers to "Keep digging" and then turned to us.

"Well?" I greeted him. "How goes the fight?"

When Harris closed the door, his demeanor changed. He almost seemed like a kid in a candy store. I was getting the impression he might like us.

"I gotta hand it to you," he said. "You kicked the hell out of this hornet nest."

"What do you mean?" Tom asked, taking a sharp breath as he adjusted and his shoulder had to move in the sling.

"Your *investigation*. I'm sorry for suspecting you out of the gate. I should have had you working with me from go. Come see me if the whole band thing doesn't work out for you three. We could use you here."

"Apology accepted, Detective." I smiled at him. "What's going on? There's a lot of action still happening around here."

"Yeah." He broke into a bigger grin. "All thanks to you. We got the go-ahead to hit Big Tony's place. SWAT just got back from raiding it."

"Anything on Charlie?" I asked, leaning forward in my chair.

"Not yet," Harris said. "But we have a lot left to go through. We'll find something."

"What have you found so far?" Sam asked.

"Enough drugs to put him away for life. Also, his books had the names of every dirty cop and politician he had in his pocket." Harris was flipping through his ever-present notebook, eyes darting between it and the three of us. "We're dismantling his whole operation. This is going to be a much safer town. Hell, we're even making Canada safer."

"How so?" I asked.

"Found ties to known associates up there. Mounties already got one of them." Harris pulled a picture from one of the folders and handed it to me. He was cleaner and wearing nice clothes, but it was the dirty-looking guy I'd saved on our way out of Winnipeg. I remembered seeing snake tattoos. I just had no idea at the time to keep my eyes peeled for the snake eating its tail poking up from his shirt collar.

"Damn, they were everywhere," I said, handing the picture back. "I remember this guy. He was grimy and dirty when I saw him. He was probably swapping out the tire on the back of our van while we were on stage."

"No way you could have known." Harris tucked the picture away. "We're going to get them all, thanks to you three."

"I guess we can add crime-fighters to our resume," I said, raising my eyebrows at Tom. "We need to paint the van like the mystery machine now."

"We need to put it back together first," Tom said, discouraged.

"We can go home!" I said, turning to Harris. "We can go home, right?"

"I mean," Harris said, "it's not the best part of town, but sure. I don't think you need to worry anymore."

"No cops are going to be waiting outside this time?" Tom quipped at Harris, eyes still a little glassy.

"No promises. I might check in on you now and again." Harris smiled, slipping his little notebook back into his pocket. "I need to do a little more paperwork, and we can send you on your way."

Harris disappeared to fill out the mountains of forms it took to send someone to jail. The three of us sat exhausted in the unyielding steel chairs, Tom occasionally nodding off.

"What's next?" I asked.

"What's next for what?" Sam said, facing me.

"For us. Charlie's gone. What do we do now?"

"We keep playing," Tom said, his eyes still closed. He was slumped down in the chair, using the backrest for his head. "What else can we do?"

"It's just that Charlie has been managing all the booking details and finding the shows," I said, overwhelmed by the thought of finally returning to normal. Whatever *normal* was going to be now.

"We found our shows before. We'll do it again," Sam said. "Same as last time, someone will see us. We'll find another manager and keep booking shows."

"It's easier to get gigs when you have a drummer." Tom's eyes opened as he peered at me. "We still have a drummer, right?"

"I'm not going anywhere, but I'd like to try to do shows for more than a dozen people at a time."

"That's the plan," Tom said. "That was always the plan."

The constant bustle of activity outside the little office was never-ending. People in uniforms rushed by, getting prepared for something. I got up and walked to the open door, leaning against the frame. I turned to face down the hallway now aware that it led to holding cells.

The door opened, and two officers holding one arm each came through and started to walk their prisoner down in our direction. He lifted his head and locked eyes with me.

Big Tony.

He struggled against the guards for a moment when he saw me, a slight twitch of his upper body. Like he was thinking of charging down the hallway. The guards clamped down on him, and he relaxed. There was not much he could do with his hands behind his back and a cop on each side.

When they approached me, I nodded to them, and they stopped short of the doorway and held his arms tighter.

"You ready to tell me what happened to Charlie?" I asked.

"You won't quit, will you?" Tony's deep voice cracked a little. He had dark circles under his eyes.

"We're not giving up on this. Charlie's dead, and we almost got blamed for it. You had something to do with it." My voice was shaking with anger while I stood, eyes locked with the man I was convinced had killed my friend.

"I didn't kill your *friend*," Tony said. "How can you call him *friend* when he was using you to run my product around without you knowing it?"

"You had something on him. You must have. Charlie was a decent guy." My face went red, and my blood pressure rose.

Tony must have seen it, too; his smirk had returned. "Sure, he was an angel. It had nothing to do with all the money he got paid."

"Sarcasm is not what I need right now. I want you to tell me the truth."

"I don't care what you want or need. Because of you, I'm in cuffs." Tony's face went scarlet. "I'm not going down for a murder I didn't commit."

He tried to charge me again, but the men on either side had death grips on him, and he didn't move much. Impressive, given his size.

"I know the feeling." My turn for sarcasm. "I guess I'll have to live without a confession from you." I shrugged and nodded to the two holding him.

They dragged Tony down the hallway. He turned, still red-faced, his eyes bulging with anger. "I didn't kill Charlie, but *when* I get out, you can bet I'm coming for you."

"It's a date," I said, smiling back at Tony. "Name the time and place, and I'll be there to put you away all over again."

I headed back into the room, my body quivering with anger. I slapped my hands on the table in frustration as I sat down. "Damn it." I sighed, placing my forehead on the cold tabletop. "He's going away, but he's *getting* away with murder."

"He's never going to admit to it," Tom said. "He's a professional liar. It's literally what he does. He knows he's going down; he doesn't want the murder pinned on him, too."

"What if he isn't lying?" Sam's voice said, pulling me out of the spiral I was in.

"Then the killer is still on the loose," I said, not lifting my head off the table. "Who else could it be? There was nothing on him that led to anyone other than Tony."

"I have no idea," Sam said, her voice frustrated.

The three of us sat in the room. With no clock, time seemed to stretch on and on. The activity in the station slowed. Eventually, it was almost quiet. Someone approached. We all turned to the door as Harris entered with a pile of paperwork.

"I'm sorry that took so long," he said. "I have some things for you to sign."

The next hour was spent poring over our sworn statements. Scrawling our signatures on a hundred things, and finalizing some details of our timeline with Harris. This was the part of police work you didn't see on TV—whole forests' worth of papers for each case. *I'll stick to playing drums.*

"I know you're frustrated," Harris said once we'd finished with everything on the table. "We'll link him to it soon enough. It's only a matter of time."

"I hope you're right. It seems like Tony's even convinced himself that he's innocent."

"He's going to have plenty of time to think," Harris said with a smile. "I'll make sure to visit him and keep pressing him for more. He's going to give in and tell me the truth about Charlie, whether he likes it or not."

I sighed, knowing this was the best we would get right now. I would have loved Tony to shout about how he'd killed Charlie. I imagined the cops taking down his confession and this all being over, but Harris's promises would have to do.

The detective clapped his hands together. "Well, Bombs Away, as much as you love my smiling face, it's time for you all to leave. You're cleared of all charges."

He waited by the door when we didn't move. "Well, come on, then. If you stay here any longer, they'll charge you rent."

It was a short walk to the front of the precinct. Harris put his hand on my shoulder and thanked me again, then went back down the hallway, not one for goodbyes. As we exited through the doors, the whole precinct clapped and shouted their thanks.

Tom huffed under his breath. "They sure changed their tune."

I put my arm around his shoulders, taking care not to jostle the bad one. "You're such a cynic."

"I'm just in a bad mood," he said. "My dad will have heard about all this. Cops love to gossip. Now I gotta call him."

"You took a bullet from a gangster. You can handle calling your dad."

Tom stopped, mouth open in surprise, and smiled. "Yeah, I guess that's true. I can do anything." He stood a little straighter and threw his shoulders back to exit the station, standing tall. "Ow." He hunched back down when the motion stretched his wound. "Almost anything."

The night air slapped us back to reality. Every muscle in my body was fatigued like I'd run a marathon. I didn't remember the last time we got a restful night's sleep. "Let's go home."

Harris had called us a cab that showed up moments later. Sam and I climbed in the back, Tom up front. The driver took his time, taking the long route. I didn't care. It was on Harris's dime.

I was nodding off in the back seat when we arrived. We drove past where the showdown had just been, police tape blocking everything off. It seemed like a lifetime, but it was only a few hours ago.

We pulled up to our door and piled out. Our shitty warehouse had never been so inviting. We marched inside and up the stairs to the old office, collapsing into our various sleeping spaces. After days of running all over the city, gunfights, car chases, arrests, sting operations, and more gunfights, I closed my eyes.

Sleep hit me before I was even covered up.

It was over. It was finally done.

Chapter 22

Tuesday, November 11th, 1986, 1:00 p.m.

We stomped our feet as we entered the building. The little place represented the last of our money. Looking around, I saw that it wasn't much, but it was exactly what we needed.

With winter approaching, the temperature had dropped, and we couldn't rehearse at home. We had enough trouble keeping our living space warm, and the rest of the warehouse worked better as a refrigerator than a rehearsal venue.

This place was warm. The walls were painted a cheery blue, peeling in some spots, but not bad. Music memorabilia was hidden in every nook and cranny they could find. A few older instruments hung on the walls or leaned in a corner.

We lugged what little equipment we had with us and started to set up. This would work for practicing for our show. I was excited about our first gig since Winnipeg.

Sam must have gotten sick of Tom and me moping around sometime in early October. We had watched her walk over and pick up the phone. She dialed a number and stared at us the whole time. It had to have been ringing.

The only thing I had been able make out was something that sounded like an adult in a Charlie Brown cartoon coming from the other end of the phone. Sam had conversed with them easily. She turned her back to us, speaking almost inaudibly into the receiver. I was only able to make out a few words. *Show. Publicity. Charlie.*

She'd pivoted to face us after hanging up the phone. "It's time to start practicing. We've got a November slot at The Palms. Now off your asses, and let's go to work."

Easy as that, Sam had called The Palms and convinced them we deserved the slot Charlie had gotten for us. They agreed, and they also decided it would be a draw to see the punk band that had been arrested for and cleared of murder.

We began rehearsing right away until it got too cold to continue at the warehouse. We spent the rest of what little money we had on this rehearsal space.

"One, two, three, four!" I said, slapping my drumsticks together.

We rolled into one of the new songs we'd been working on. It was not quite there yet, but it was close. I could safely say we'd be ready to bring the roof down by the time the gig rolled around. We were better than ever before—a second chance would do that for you. We sat catching our breath after the song, taking a moment before launching into the next one when the door crashed open.

"Guess who's come to join the party!" a familiar voice called out as they entered the room.

Mick stood before us, holding a pistol at his side, almost, but not quite pointing it in our direction.

"You couldn't just go away?" he asked us. "You couldn't pack up and find some other town?" He waved the gun around, talking with his hands.

"Mick." Standing behind my kit I had my hands in the air, a drumstick in each. "What's with the piece? What's going on?"

"I had the perfect setup. Everything was going fine." He aimed directly at me. "Why couldn't you just give up and go to jail? You had to turn into Columbo?"

We hadn't seen Mick since the day he'd sold us out to Big Tony. There had been no news of him either. We'd told Harris all about it, but it was like Mick had disappeared off the face of the earth.

"We'd hoped you'd be the one to give up," I told him. His arm snapped up, and the barrel was now leveled at my head. "Big Tony's in jail, Mick. What are you doing here?"

"Loose ends. I don't need you screwing things up again."

Out of the corner of my eye, I saw Sam circling Mick while he was focused on me.

"Let's all relax." I raised my hands further and took a couple of steps in Mick's direction.

"Stop moving!" he yelled. "You've taken everything from me!"

My confusion was growing. We only knew Mick from seeing him at clubs and hanging out with him once or twice. He would help us set up for shows, knew his way around all the equipment, and used to have a band. I couldn't remember ever taking anything from him except some free beer.

"We have no idea what you're talking about."

"My band." His eyes were wild and filled with rage. "We were Charlie's first clients. We were the ones who started bringing the drugs into town for him. When Steve got hooked, Charlie stopped getting us gigs in Canada. Steve OD'd not long after that, and it all started to fall apart."

Mick was standing, his eyes trained on me, but I didn't think he saw anything. He was lost in the story he was telling. Sam inched around, trying not to draw his attention.

"Then *you* come along." Mick jabbed his pistol to punctuate his rant. "All bright-eyed and naive. Charlie scooped you up and started giving you all our gigs. Big Tony had taken over by that point, and Charlie was moving more product than ever, making more money than ever."

Mick's head dropped, eyes no longer meeting ours.

I took a couple steps out from behind my kit. "Mick, what are you trying to tell us?"

"What I'm trying to tell you is Tony didn't kill Charlie." He raised his arm and was now aiming back at my face. He adjusted his grip on the gun, causing me to flinch. "I did."

"What? Why?" I asked, feeling all the blood drain out of my face.

"All that money, his whole scheme—it was all *my* idea. He worked out the deal with Tony for me, but then he took *everything*."

"So you killed him?" I took another step.

Mick's head snapped up.

"Yeah, I killed him. I'm taking back what's mine. You idiots were supposed to get caught red-handed at The Palms. Then, I would make my deal and get back on Big Tony's good side. Find a new band and start again. Instead, you ran off before the cops showed up."

"You're insane. This is over. It's done. Big Tony's gone." I had my hands up in front of me, an ineffective shield against the bullet Mick wanted to send my way.

"Actually, I wanted to thank you for that. With Tony out of the picture, a vacancy opened that I intend to fill. I'll take over the whole thing, find another stupid band to run my dope for me. You've done me a favor."

"Don't thank us yet," I said and nodded to Sam.

She swung her bass at Mick as he turned toward what I was nodding at. The gun went off as she hit Mick's arm, forcing it to point at the floor. There was a whine as the bullet ricocheted off the tiles and a sting as it grazed my cheek.

The pistol clattered past me as it flew out of Mick's most likely broken hand. He hugged it to his body and screamed at Sam, "You stupid bitch! You assholes ruin everything!"

Mick howled in pain and anger, lunging at Sam.

Sam stepped to one side and swatted him away. Like water flowing in a stream, one minute she was in front of him, then Mick was on the ground.

He stood up, eyes wild, still cradling his right arm. Tom was right beside him. Mick threw a left and connected with Tom's jaw. With a grunt, Tom fell to one knee.

After all we had been through, Tom was not as meek as he used to be. He wiped the blood from the corner of his mouth and pushed off the ground. He stood, his arm flailing into an uppercut that connected with Mick's chin, snapping his head back. He stumbled a few steps, right into me. I shoved him away, and he staggered into the corner, hitting the wall.

As he turned back to me, there was a clatter of metal on the tile floor. Mick's feet had found the gun. He reached down to grab it and spun around with the weapon back in his hands lined up with my chest.

The crack of a gunshot filled the air. I flinched, my hand coming up to my chest and expecting to feel pain and blood running through my fingers. I looked at my hand—no blood.

A gurgle drew my attention. Mick, pistol still in hand, fell to his knees. He glanced down at his gun in confusion, then to the front of his shirt, where a bloodstain bloomed larger and larger. With a final gasp, he collapsed flat on his face.

"You three have the worst luck," Harris said, stepping the rest of the way into the room. "What the hell is going on here?"

I release my hand from my chest after realizing I was still clutching it. "Well, you got Charlie's killer."

Harris holstered his pistol and walked up to Mick. He kicked the weapon away from him and knelt, checking his pulse. "I'm going to need to call this in. Is there a phone in this place?"

I gestured to the back wall. Harris made his way over and rang the station. After a brief conversation, he hung it back up and turned to us. "I guess you're going to have to cut rehearsal short. What happened here?"

We explained the last few minutes and everything Mick had revealed to us. Harris nodded along, scribbling in his trusty notebook.

"Would you look at that? We are lucky, after all," I said after finishing all the details. "Lucky you showed up."

"Yeah," Tom said. "Why are you here?"

"Your dad told me where you'd be."

In the aftermath of what we went through, Tom had called his dad, and he was right about all cops knowing each other in this town. He and Harris were friends enough now that they were checking in with each other.

"Something come up with the case?" I asked.

"You could say that." Harris nodded. "Big Tony was murdered in his cell."

The shocked silence in the room grew.

"What happened?" I asked once I was able to find words again.

"We're not sure yet, but if I had to wager a guess, it probably had something to do with your friend here."

Harris crossed the room to an empty trash bin and pulled out the plastic used to line it. Using it like a glove, he picked up the gun off the floor and gently placed it on a shelf—a useless gesture since Mick was in no condition to go for it. It seemed to make Harris feel better, though.

"So, it's over?" Tom asked. "It's really over this time?"

A few uniformed men came in through the open door. They gathered evidence and statements, took pictures, and eventually carried the body away. The owners of the rehearsal space came and were talked to by the police. They refunded our money and politely asked us to find somewhere else to practice.

We gathered up our equipment and made our way out of the building with Harris.

"I think it's safe to say that this is over," he said, looking at Tom.

Tom took a deep breath and blew it out. A weight had lifted from all of us, one I didn't think we'd realized was still there.

"Do me a favor." Harris smiled at us. "Stay out of trouble, would you?"

"That's the thing, Detective," I replied. "We never went looking for it in the first place."

"Well, it sure seemed to find you."

"How about this," I said, holding my hand out to the detective to seal the deal. "We'll do our damndest to avoid any, but if it finds us again, we'll call you first."

"Deal." Harris shook each of our hands in turn. As he climbed into his car, he called out, "Good luck at your show. I've got my ticket already, but I may or may not be wearing earplugs."

We waved to Harris as he pulled away. I felt energized, like the air was charged with possibility. For the first time in a couple of months, there was no looming threat, no danger.

I knew The Palms would go well. I could feel it. This was our time, our chance. Tom and Sam were both smiling. They knew it, too. Our future before us, exciting and utterly ours.

Chapter 23

Saturday, June 27th, 1987, 8:47 p.m.

The drums and bass from the first opening band rumbled the floor beneath our feet. Flashes of light illuminated our faces with random colors. Backstage was cramped and stank of sweat and beer, but it was alive, electric with anticipation. Whenever the music paused, a roar from the crowd washed over us. They were hungry and waiting for more. I tapped my drumstick against my leg in time with the song, the room's pulse syncing up with my own.

"You ready for this?" Tom shouted, his towering mohawk now colored like a sunset, reds fading to orange at the tips. He shifted his weight from foot to foot, the jitters making him do his awkward pre-show dance. It was the same dance he'd done before every time he'd go on stage.

Sam nodded to him, standing there like some punk rock goddess. Her bass slung over her shoulder; her hair so blond now it was almost white. In her eyes, a storm was brewing. She was focused, ready to bring the house down.

Tom turned to me and inclined his chin in a "how about you" motion.

"Born ready," I shot back, giving him a grin that felt like the edges touched my ears.

The song beyond the curtains and the drumsticks on my leg picked up the pace. The song crept closer to a crescendo, like a balloon with too much water ready to pop.

My mind wandered. It was hard to believe it had been almost a year. I glanced around the backstage area. It was small but new and clean, and the floor was hardly sticky. Beyond the curtain was a brand-new outdoor amphitheater that could hold more people than I thought we'd ever be in front of. I remembered all the dives, a dozen people in the audience, and a few dollars in our pockets at the end of the night.

After Charlie, it was like starting over. Sam had been like a bulldog, finding us gigs wherever she could. That first one at The Palms didn't go as well as we'd hoped. With what happened to Charlie there, the owners had sold it. We had no idea, but the new management had turned it into a strip club. I've never seen Tom blush so much, it had to be a new record. Even though it wasn't a great start we kept going anyway, keeping up the hustle.

I focused on what was happening around me, and the music swept back in, still building, still thumping away beyond the curtains. Sam and Tom were staring at me, and I could tell the same things were running through their heads.

After that, Sam got us another gig and then another. Anywhere that would take us. Some places weren't even expecting a punk band. Not everything was perfect, and one went wrong real fast: a rough-and-tumble country bar. We didn't realize until it was too late. The only thing that saved us was the chain-link fence that separated us from the unwashed masses. It did its job catching the beer bottles that flew at the stage.

A few months later, after we'd been doing the rounds for a while, the right person finally caught our act. A small producer approached us after we played and helped us cut a demo. Everything changed once Rudy recorded that tape and put it in our hands.

The shows started coming faster. We had actual recorded music to give to club owners. They heard us, and more and more of them wanted us to do a show. Eventually, our tape found its way to a radio station. WSME put our song in heavy rotation. I remembered hearing "Detonate" one day, walking down the street—our tune blasting out of someone's stereo.

After that, people started to call and find us. We weren't hunting for gigs anymore. More people showed up in the crowds, too. Somewhere along the way, we got to the point where we couldn't do the small clubs we started in. They no longer had enough space.

It still blew my mind—Bombs Away selling out shows. I had to keep reminding myself that this was just the beginning. We had to keep pushing and keep going. We were doing great in the Midwest, getting gigs from Michigan to Minnesota, but beyond that, not many people knew who we were. Today, we were looking to change that.

"It's been a hell of a year," I said, projecting my voice over the music blaring around us.

Tom acknowledged me with a grin. Sam gave a curt nod. I was shocked; she was nervous, too.

"There's a lot of people out there," she said, adjusting her curtain of hair, making sure it covered as much of her face as possible.

"We've got this," Tom said, clapping Sam and me on the shoulder. "This is what we've been waiting for."

"You're positive there are record execs here?" I asked him, even though he'd been talking about it all week.

"Yeah, man," he replied. "Rudy told me he got the demo to a few that said they'd be here. He doesn't make shit like that up."

The band before us was doing one final song, so we shifted around, unable to contain our excitement and anticipation. The waiting made it feel even more cramped. We could have stepped down and backed off the stage for some breathing room, but there was something about waiting in the wings.

I tried to peek around to see how many people were watching the show. The angle was terrible, and the lights made everything beyond the band a sea of darkness. I could hear the crowds milling outside, walking past us to see some other band.

Summerfest. The word rolled around in my brain. At this point, Summerfest had been going on for almost twenty years. Some of the biggest bands in the world had come through here. There were tons of stages and eight days of music, and our little band was set to open for one of the headliners.

I still wasn't sure how it all transpired. The demo did well. We got some radio time, more shows, and then boom, we were opening for The Bangles.

A loud crash of drums and guitars signaled the end of the last song for the first opening band. They came pouring off into the wings, and we squeezed aside to make room for them to head out. We all nodded to each other like we knew a secret, trying to play it cool. Inside, I knew they must be as giddy as we were. We should be high-fiving and screaming about how amazing this was.

Our anticipation built, and one of the local radio station DJs made his way out in front of the audience. I craned my neck around the curtains to see him illuminated in the spotlight but nothing else.

"You may have heard these next folks on my show," the DJ shouted into the microphone. "They're from right here in Milwaukee. When they're not being accused of murder, they find time to make some music."

He was met with silence. They weren't here for us, but we hoped we could make an impression so they'd never forget.

I adjusted the drumsticks in my hands and checked that I had another pair in my back pocket. I saw Sam and Tom adjusting the straps on their instruments, trying to find something to do to calm the nerves.

"So, give a warm hometown welcome to the one, the only, Bombs Away!"

The crowd gave a polite cheer as we ran out to take our places. I got behind the drumkit, and the others took their places on either side, plugging their instruments in. The cheers died down. I looked up from my kit as the pulsing and sweeping lights briefly illuminated the amphitheater.

Twenty thousand faces stared back at me. I was stunned. Never in my wildest dreams could I have imagined what this would be like. Adrenaline pumped through my veins.

Tom turned and gave me a "how the hell did we get here?" face. Sam adjusted her strap again and then made sure her hair was still just right. I'd seen her go up against people twice her size in the last few years. It seemed like she could do anything, but I guess everyone got nervous.

"Hello, Milwaukee!" Tom screamed into the microphone.

The crowd erupted, cheers and feet stomping. It hit me like a wave, crashing over me and threatening to knock me down.

"This is wild. Last week, a packed house was a couple hundred people. Look at us now! Thanks for coming out to hear some music!"

He was in his element. He stood confident, sure of himself, and commanding the stage. How the tables had turned.

"So, how about it? You ready, Milwaukee?" Shouts and whistles made their way to the stage. "I'm Tom. I'll be singing and strumming this guitar. That's Sam. She'll bring the bass." Tom turned and pointed at me. "Over there on drums, that's Sticks. Let's go!"

I clapped my sticks together, and we launched into our first song. We had some new ones that were proving to go over a little better for a larger audience. Songs that got you on your feet, pumping your fists in the air.

It was hard to hear anything beyond our instruments, and I was blind to anything beyond my kit as soon as the spotlights hit me, so it was hard to judge how the crowd was feeling. The first song wound down and ended with a crash of cymbals.

There was silence for a moment. My mind was racing. They didn't like it.

Then the crowd erupted with cheers, stomping feet, and some sharp whistles called out from the dark.

"That was 'Tightrope.' How about another?" Tom called out.

The applause slammed into us like a physical thing, a wall of sound.

We launched into our next song and poured our hearts into it. Everything we had, all our frustrations over the last year. The ups, the downs, all of it. Sweat started to pour down my face. The humid summer air wrapped around me like a blanket.

When the song was over, we stared wide-eyed at each other, grinning. The cheers were louder this time. Sam was back to her old self. The rush of the performance had her in her element.

"One more song, and we'll get our sorry asses off the stage to make room for who you're here for! You've been amazing. Thank you, Milwaukee!" Tom's fist rose high in the air while he spoke to the darkness before him. "This is called, 'Detonate.'"

If I thought the cheers were loud before, this was another level. It was physical, visceral. It echoed in every corner of the stadium.

"Sounds like you know this one," Tom said and launched into the song.

This was a night of firsts. We'd played the clubs; we had some fans now. Sometimes, we could see them mouthing the words to our songs. This was different. It was like all twenty thousand people were singing along. We could hear it, our song washing over us as an ensemble of voices sang it back to us.

Tom stopped strumming his guitar when we were about to go into the chorus. He walked to the front and sang the last line of the bridge. He held the microphone out over the edge with his other hand cupped to his ear, the lights illuminating his hair and setting it alight.

The audience sang the entire chorus without hesitation. The sound of all those voices singing our song was something I'd never forget.

Tom circled back to the microphone stand and clipped it in. He swung his guitar up from his side and launched into the last verse. He was strumming the final power chords on his guitar. He walked over to the elevated platform my drums were on and stepped up onto it. He gave me a single nod, still strumming, then leaped, turning around to face the amphitheater. When his feet hit the ground, he played the final chord as I slammed the last time on the drums.

Thunderous approval shook the stage.

"Thank you again, Milwaukee!" Tom yelled into the mic, both fists in the air.

The cheers continued to build. I saw Tom reaching down to unplug his guitar so we could make way for the crew to prepare for the main act. He stopped and raised his head, looking over the amphitheater, taking it all in one last time.

A light in the dark, then another, flickering flames illuminating twenty thousand faces. They spread through the whole amphitheater—a constellation of tiny yellow and orange stars flickering before us.

It happened slowly at first. Then, increasing in volume, a chant.

"One more!" Feet stomped. "One more. One more. One more."

Tom turned to me and shrugged, then turned back to the microphone. "Ask, and you shall receive," he said, a smile spreading across his face. "This is a new one. I think you'll like it."

I turned to the microphone mounted next to me and called out while clapping my sticks together, "Bombs Away! One, two, three, four!"

Afterwards

Sunday, June 28th, 1987, 3:57 a.m.

—SAM—

The ringing in my ears hadn't stopped. It pounded on my skull, a relentless echo of the final chord we struck. It didn't bother me. I loved it. It was proof this night had happened, that Bombs Away brought the house down. My fingers twitched, the thrum of my bass strings still buzzing through my whole body as I sat on the corner of my bed.

Through my open door, Tom and Sticks were lying dead to the world, crashed in exhausted heaps on the couch and cot. Tom was hugging his pillow like a long-lost love. Sticks, sprawled out on his cot, was snoring so loud you'd think he was trying to outdo the volume of his drums.

I couldn't sleep, not yet. I felt too wired to get any rest. I shifted and glanced around the place. Nervous energy made me want to do something, stay moving. My whole body buzzed, as if electricity was sparking just beneath my skin.

I lay back on the bed, hair falling back from the side of my face that was always covered. It was okay. No one was looking. I reached up to trace my fingers along the scar. It ran from my temple to the bottom of my ear. It was only a thin line now, not as visible as it used to be.

Memories long buried rose to the surface—another life, a long time ago.

This life, this new life, was something else. America, the land of the free, home of the brave, all that jazz. It never occurred to me that I would find this life here, stumble onto my purpose, and find a place and a family to belong to. Guilt flashed through me like lightning.

I don't deserve this. The thought rattled around in my brain like it always did.

I tried never to let it show, never let anyone see past the shields I put up—not even the boys. I didn't think they'd like what they'd find. I forced the guilt down. We were doing well here. Tonight was a good night. I couldn't let the past cloud that. The three of us had worked hard. We deserved this.

Another thrill shot through me. So many people had seen me up there. I bolted upright in panic, causing the bed springs to protest with a squeak. I combed my hair over my scar with my fingers. I took deep, calming breaths to slow my heart rate again. *It's okay, Sam. No one knows you here. You're safe.*

Everything slowed down, and the panic passed. My mind was still on our performance—all those people cheering, cheering for our music, something we'd been waiting for. We'd finally done it.

I slumped back onto the bed again. My body relaxed enough to start drifting. The ringing in my ears was muffled now.

The shrill sound of the telephone tore through the apartment's silence. I shot up, scrambling out of bed and padded to the receiver. I picked it up and put it to my ear, cursing whoever was calling this early in the morning. A glance at the boys told me they hadn't noticed. They were still out cold.

I hadn't had a chance to say anything into the phone when someone spoke.

"Samantha?"

I froze. I knew that voice.

"No." I hung up the phone and took a cautious step back, staring at it like it was a viper about to strike.

It rang again, the sound erupting around me. One ring. I waited to see if it woke the boys. No response. A second ring. No response. On the third ring, Sticks let out a snore and shifted in his sleep. I had to answer it, or it would rouse him.

I reached out and grabbed the receiver, bringing it to my ear. "Yeah?"

"Samantha Varavyova?" The voice on the other end was clear, deep, and familiar.

A heavy feeling settled in my gut, a mix of apprehension and something darker. "Who's asking?"

"I'm hurt," the voice said. "Have you forgotten me already? After all I did for you?"

"Agent Curtis." The name tasted like regret. A life left behind, a life I thought I was done with.

"Ah. I'm glad I'm not completely forgotten after all. How are you, Samantha?"

"It's just Sam," I corrected automatically, a reflex born from years of taking on this new life.

"Of course, Sam. My mistake."

The smug way he said my name pissed me off even more. "What do you want?" I stepped back into my room with the long, coiled cord unraveling and stretching behind me. I shut the door, trapping the cord but blocking some of the sound of this pre-dawn conversation.

"Well, Sam, it's been years, but the uncle you're named after needs you. We're calling in the favor you owe us."

"I didn't realize I owed you anything else. I gave you everything. I burned my life down to stay in this country."

"And we're grateful for that." Curtis was now all business, no smile in his voice. "But we need one last thing. The US government needs your help."

"It's been years. What could you need from me?"

"I should rephrase that. We need help from you *and* your band."

I couldn't speak. That wasn't my life anymore. Now they wanted to drag me *and* the boys into something, too?

"What could you possibly want them for?" I asked when I was able to find my words again.

"Well, after your amazing show last night, you are going to get a call. Congratulations, you're getting a record deal."

"What? How could you know that?"

"First of all," he drawled, sounding cocky, "the United States government knows everything. Also, we may have called in a favor to expedite this for you."

The ringing in my ears increased in volume, but I didn't think it was the concert this time. Waves of fear and anger crashed over me. The feeling that my life was no longer my own. I didn't like that at all, and that was the reason I left home so long ago. Now here I sat, getting sucked right back into it again.

"Along with that shiny new recording contract, you'll be going on tour," Curtis said, sounding like he was awarding us the lottery. "You'll have stops all over the United States, then move on to Europe. You'll be touring for a couple of years."

"I still haven't heard the favor you need me to do." I injected as much venom into the word *favor* as possible.

"Don't rush. We're getting there. Before you go overseas, we'll send you a passport with a new last name. We wouldn't want anyone to know you're coming home. Hell, we'll even leave the last name off it. Just 'Sam,' as you're so fond of saying."

Panic gripped me, my body trembling with anxiety. I knew all those years ago that someday, my old life might come back to bite me, but I didn't realize they'd been tracking me the whole time. They'd been watching and listening. So much for all that freedom I was promised in exchange.

"So, what do you need us to do?" I asked.

"Well, first thing's first: your bandmates can't find out about this. They just need to play their instruments and sing your little songs."

The anger simmering in my belly began to boil. Our *little songs* were the cover he needed for whatever this was. He needed to give us a little more respect. I opened my mouth to say something, then closed it again. It wasn't going to change his mind. Curtis didn't care about what we did anyway. He probably listened to Barry Manilow on repeat.

"When you three are in Europe, we'll be in touch with more instructions," he said. "The temperature in your old home is changing. More and more people are being let back in. The security is relaxing, especially for artists and musicians."

"How long have you been planning this?"

"Oh." The damned cockiness was back in his voice again. "A long time. When security finally began to relax, we started trying to find opportunities. Then we realized a band would be the perfect cover."

"I'm assuming I don't have a choice in all this?" I already knew the answer.

"You always have a choice. You can go home to work for us, or you can get dragged back when someone finds out where you are." The threat in his words was clear as day. *Work for them or die.* "You'll hit all the concert stops in Europe. We'll give you more instructions before your tour takes you home."

"How exactly do you plan for me to go home? Someone will spot me eventually." Curtis was underestimating how many bridges I'd burned on my way out.

"Oh, we've got it all worked out. There's going to be a festival in a year or so. We're getting it all arranged. Tons of huge acts—the perfect opportunity for an up-and-coming band to tag along. Everyone's eyes will be on the headliners. No one will be paying attention to the smaller acts."

"So you think we'll be able to roll up in tour buses?" I was torn between anger and, deep down, excitement. Bombs Away on tour all over America and Europe, a music festival. The boys were going to lose their minds.

"Yeah, that's exactly what we think. You'll roll up in the buses, everyone will be so excited to see Ozzy Osborne and..." Curtis paused. "What the hell kind of name is this? Mötley Crüe? They didn't even spell it right."

"Nice to know your finger is on the pulse, Curtis."

My jab didn't faze him. He acted like I hadn't said anything at all.

"Anyway, with all eyes on them, you'll slip into the country and take care of what we need. Then slip back out."

"You make it sound so easy." Surely he knew it was going to be anything but easy, but he probably didn't care as long as he got what he wanted.

The struggle in me was reaching a fever pitch. I was being forced into this. I could run, disappear. I'd done it before, and I could do it again. My hand was poised to slam the receiver down and bolt out the door—

Sticks snored from the other room. Springs creaked as Tom turned over in his sleep.

I couldn't leave them. They were my family now, the only family I had.

"When do we start?" I asked.

"We'll be in touch. Someone will call later today with the news about the contract and the tour. Try to act surprised."

"I'll do my best," I deadpanned.

"I know you will," Curtis said dryly. "After that, enjoy your music. Make a record, go on tour. We'll reach out when the time is right."

"So, pretend like this call never happened?"

"That's it. We'll reach out a few days before the festival to arrange everything."

My stomach sank. Once again, I was not in control. Just when things were going well, the rug got pulled out from under me. I decided I'd go along with it to keep the boys safe, to stay alive.

"Oh, and Sam," Curtis said. "How's your Russian?"

The line clicked, and the dial tone rang out of the receiver, harmonizing with the sound already echoing in my head.

I was going home. "Zhizn' ebet meya."

-- Bombs Away will return. --

Scan the QR code to stream the 1988 single "Detonate" by Bombs Away!!

If your steaming service is not at the link above. Just
search for: Detonate by Bombs Away!! wherever you get
your music.

<u>**Acknowledgements**</u>

A special thanks to my wife Monica and my son Flynn. I appreciate your never ending support and belief that I could finally put some words on paper and write this book!

Thank you to my editor Clara for turning my mess of a manuscript into something people actually may want to read.

Thank you to Charley for bringing the sound of Bombs Away to life.